I0847574

KISS MY SASS

C.D. GORRI

KISS MY SASS

Dire Wolf Mates 6
by C.D. Gorri
Edited by BookNookNuts

Copyright 2023 C.D. Gorri, NJ

For Tammy,
Thank you for your unwavering support and always
being straight with me.
Xoxo, C.D.

Before you begin sign up for my newsletter here:
SUBSCRIBE HERE

This is a work of fiction. All of the characters,

names, places, organizations, and events portrayed in this novel are either part of the author's imagination and/or used fictitiously and are not to be construed as real. Any resemblance to any person, living or dead, actual events, locales or organizations is entirely coincidental. This eBook is licensed for your personal enjoyment only. All rights are reserved. No part of this book is to be reproduced, scanned, downloaded, printed, or distributed in any manner whatsoever without written permission from the author. Please do not participate in or encourage piracy of any m

BLURB

Can a Dire Wolf with *the sight* find his future with a wanted female?

Rare Raven Shifter Domenica Corvo is being hunted by her ex, the leader of her former Murder, when she stumbles on her knight in shining fur.

Thor Ulger is not just the Enforcer for the Dire Wolf MC. He is also their Seer—an ancient and feared position gifted by the Fates to those strong enough to hold it.

Part of his job is to see the paths of those Wolves he calls Pack, and to mark their skin with their stories once they have found their fated mates. If only he was destined for the same future as those he cares about.

Resigned to living his life alone, Thor's entire

world turns upside down when a Raven with a broken wing crash lands at his feet. She needs sanctuary, but this sassy little bird is no one's pet project.

He thought falling in love wasn't in the cards, but the Fates work in mysterious ways. Thor is on the fast track to losing his heart with every passing second.

When her ex demands she return to him, there's only one answer as far as Thor is concerned.

Anyone coming for his mate can *kiss his sass*!

PROLOGUE

Thor's head pounded, and exhaustion filled his veins. He could hardly muster the strength to return the cheers and congratulations floating about the Pack House tonight.

It was always the same when the sight took over. Thor was present, but not. The tattoo he'd inked across Weylin's body showed a promising future for the male and his newly awakened she-Wolf mate.

He was glad for Gwen and Weylin. Just as he was glad for his Alpha and Alpha fem. He'd even performed the ceremony, marrying the couple just minutes before Lucy and Derrick welcomed their three precious cubs into the world.

Tonight was a good night. Fuck yes, it was. But instead of being happy, Thor felt completely and utterly drained. He ducked out of the Pack House for some much needed quiet time, walking to the end of the paved lot that bumped up against some woods.

He still could not believe this was all theirs. Their bar, their house, their land. At first, when Derrick had suggested pooling their resources and settling down to establish roots, Thor had been uncertain. The Dire Wolf MC was built on the belief that their kind did better on the road.

Sure, there were different branches, and yes, they technically still belonged to the main MC, which was a human term for the motorcycle loving Shifters. Really, their MC was a Pack. An ancient, powerful Pack made up of prehistoric monsters like Thor, whose Dire Wolves needed the freedom of the road lest they be drawn into petty wars with other supernaturals.

It was the nature of the beast, he knew. Shifters, especially, were nothing if not predictable. Volatile creatures, they thrived on physical violence and the establishment of a hierarchy. Everyone wanted to be the toughest, strongest, and most lethal. Reputation was everything, and fortunately or unfortunately, depending on how you saw it, the Dire Wolves had quite the rep for being badasses. Which made everyone and their motherfucking uncle want to challenge them.

So far, so good.

The Dire Wolves hadn't had to deal with any threats, but that could also be because the Wolf world was blowing up left and right with the demand for a High Alpha. So involved in their own politics, the local Macconwood Pack Wolves had left the Dire Wolves to themselves. Their Alpha was a good male, a worthy male, and the one meeting they'd had established the fact he was uninterested in challenging Derrick for anything.

Settling down had been a good move on Derrick's part. Perfect, really. Most of the Pack had paired up and Thor had his job to do. But nothing could fill the hole he felt inside him. Thor crouched down, trailing his fingers across the ground as he sucked in a long, deep breath.

Fuck. What a day.

SO much for being a Seer. Thor had no inkling his long time Pack mate and friend, Weylin, would come to him to perform their most sacred and ancient tattooing ritual. A good thing, for sure, but typically he had a clue when he was about to dive into the ether.

But the decision was not up to Thor. It was up to

the Fates. This was the way it happened for their kind. When a Dire Wolf found his or her fated mate, it was up to the Pack Seer to convey the story of them on the Dire Wolf's back.

Thor used special magicked ink gifted to their MC by friends of the Pack. It was the only kind strong enough to penetrate Dire Wolf skin, and bamboo pens to inscribe the picture as was given to him by the Spirits.

He was touched by the gods. One of the few Dire Wolves to inherit *the sight.* He was the Seer. That meant it was Thor's job to perform such duties. But communing with the spirit guides of their ancestors took its toll on him, and each time he went under, he felt the desire to return to the natural world lessen more and more.

If it wasn't for his bonds to his Pack and Alpha, Thor might still be there in the *other world,* walking and talking amongst the ghosts of the past. He shivered involuntarily, looking up at the bright September moon.

The month was almost over, and soon fall would be in full effect. No more lazy summer nights and warm breezes. Fall and winter would be especially hard this year. He should know. His grandfather,

Bjorn Ulger, had told him all about it on this recent visit with the old graybeard's spirit.

Ghost wasn't a term the deceased liked, and Thor knew better than to use it to describe the corporeally challenged. Bodies turned to dust, but spirits were eternal. If anything, Thor had that to comfort him.

Still, he rubbed his chest, the feeling of something coming heavy on his mind. Funny, really. He figured the *something coming* had happened already. After he'd tattooed Weylin and subsequently passed out, Derrick's mate, Lucy, had gone into labor.

Good thing Thor had bookmarked that webpage he'd seen on how to get your license to perform marriages in under ten minutes. Derrick had also done his part, getting the license ahead of time, knowing the fury of his mate if he failed to marry her before their cubs came into the world.

He grinned tiredly as he pictured a panting, grunting Lucy with tears in her eyes and a curse for her mate on her lips as he presented her with the document. She'd just had to sign then repeat after Thor, and bam! The two of them were married. A couple of hours later, three brand new cubs were born.

Three cubs. Three precious lives. Three girls.

Thor shook his head. He didn't know whether to laugh or cry for Derrick. The man was one lucky sonovabitch in his opinion. But of that feeling of some impending doom or greatness—*it was still a toss-up which*—hadn't ebbed with the coming of the triplets.

"What is it?" he grumbled.

Asking his grandfather for help on this plane was pretty pointless, but he did it anyway, keeping his voice low and deep. Thor stood, knowing there were no answers incoming.

He turned away from the woods, about to head back to the House, to his room where he would spend yet another night tossing and turning in his big, empty bed. He paused. Frozen mid-step, Thor noticed something hurtling towards him from the sky.

"What the hell?"

The thing was small and dark and traveling unbelievably fast. He squinted, watching its progression before it nosedived a few hundred feet away. Thor didn't know why, but he took off running towards the falling object. He had to get there, had to help.

It was a biological imperative. Thor growled, pulling on his Wolf's strength to up his speed. He slid the last fifteen feet just in time to catch the thing before it could crash into the hard asphalt. He was out of breath, heart thundering, when he opened his big hands to see a giant black bird cradled against his body.

A raven. A female raven.

CHAPTER I

She smelled like clean rain on a crisp Autumn day. Like freshly baked bread and sweet summer jam. The Raven smelled good. Too good.

He frowned as he looked at the small creature. Impossibly dark, glossy feathers trembled as the animal loosed a pitiful cry. She was in pain, and the knowledge caused something dark to grow inside of his mind. Something or someone had hurt her, and Thor's Demon Wolf snarled in fury.

The bird was covered in scratches and blood. His growl escaped his lips. He noted the odd way the Raven's wing was bent and was careful not to jostle her unnecessarily. How had she flown with that?

Fuck. Worry replaced his anger at whoever had

done this to the creature. He could not imagine the pain she was in.

Poor, brave, determined thing.

"Shhh. It's okay. I got you," he whispered, needing to console the sweet-smelling bird.

For some reason, his voice would not come out any louder. He didn't think too deeply about that. Just held her gently, crooning stuff and nonsense, trying to settle the animal.

Not animal. Ours, his Demon Wolf murmured inside his mind's eye.

Thor froze, then he felt it. Magic. Shifter magic. The vibration was familiar, and his eyes narrowed, zeroing in on the Raven in his hands. The black bird's body was larger than a wild raven's would be. She was already warm, but started growing warmer as the vibration grew stronger.

He narrowed his eyes, taking in the blue black aura swirling around her body. Oh fuck. Surprise and awe filled him when, suddenly, instead of a bird, Thor was holding a woman. Her lush body felt good in his arms, but he wasn't about to overstep any Shifter niceties by paying attention to the side of his brain screaming at him to look his fill.

Instead, his eyes remained on her face, willing hers to open. Finally, they did, and stole his very breath from his chest. Clear and blue, her eyes flashed up at him, and Thor sucked in another sharp breath. It was like he'd forgotten to breathe.

His lungs were burning, but he couldn't seem to get any oxygen. Her eyes were gorgeous, stunning, rooting him where he sat. They reminded him of October mornings, full of promise and beauty. But that dream was short-lived. Too soon, her pretty eyes clouded over with pain, and he mourned the loss of that brightness. He wanted to punish whoever had taken it from her.

Forcing his gaze from hers, he noted a motley of bruises across her face and body. That wing, now an arm in her human skin, was dislocated if not broken. She had dozens of scratches on what was otherwise clear, smooth, fair skin with a hint of freckles on her shoulders and the bridge of her nose.

One eye was red and swollen, she would undoubtedly have a shiner by tomorrow. Her nose was bruised, and her lip cut as if she'd been punched in the face repeatedly. The fury he felt before had amplified tenfold by the time he was done cataloging her injuries.

Someone had worked her over, and his Demon Wolf snarled with the need for vengeance. The beast was not like the others in his pack. With one paw in the other world, his ideas of vengeance and loyalty were a bit more intense. But that was what happened when you were touched by the gods themselves.

"Who hurt you?" Thor asked, his voice a guttural rumble that sounded harsh to his own ears.

The female gasped as she opened her eyes. She met his bravely, and he knew he looked like one scary motherfucker with his size, his many tattoos, and his shaved head, but she didn't flinch.

Bold, beautiful, brave female. Worthy mate.

Shut the fuck up, he told his Demon Wolf.

The animal had crazy ideas about getting himself paired up, but Thor knew better. He was not made for a woman's love. His life was one of service to his Pack. That was no life for a mate. How could he ever justify putting her after the needs of his Pack mates? No. He was meant to be a lifelong loner.

"Hide me. Please, hide me," the Raven Shifter begged.

Her voice was scratchy and hoarse, as if she'd been choked, and, *motherfucker*, one look at her throat confirmed she had. Thor's rage went from simmer to boil once again, and he had to work to rein in his beast.

"Who?"

"Please, please, you have to hide me. They'll come looking!"

She gasped, panicked and in pain. Still, she leaned on him, and that puzzled Thor. A woman who'd been roughed up by some lesser males would surely push him away, but she didn't. Instead, she used her one good arm to cling to him instead.

Good. Ours.

Thor ignored his animal. Focused on the woman, he needed to know more about her situation so he could protect her.

"Who? Who is after you?" he asked again.

Thor watched helplessly as those gorgeous eyes rolled back inside her head as she passed out in his arms. Shit. What was he supposed to do now?

"Fucking hell," he growled, not for any other reason than because he wanted to protect her.

He didn't understand why, but the feeling was damn near overwhelming. Thor stood, holding the woman in his arms. She moaned softly, and he moderated his pace to not jostle her any more than necessary.

The rest of the Pack was likely just getting to bed after all the excitement, but he needed them now. Pulling on his bonds, he called on Brock, the Pack

Beta. By the time Thor got to the pack door, the male was there waiting with it open.

"Who is she?" Brock asked, carefully averting his gaze away from her naked body.

Good. Thor was feeling volatile as fuck, and though Brock technically outranked him, he was glad the man was already claimed and mated to a curvy little Lioness. The fact he had looked away was clearly him trying to assuage Thor's stress.

Fuck. Don't get attached. She is not mine.

Yes, she is, his Demon Wolf disagreed.

"Bro, you need to calm down," Brock said, brows furrowed.

"What?"

"Stop growling before you wake the whole house."

Damn. Was he actually growling? Thor shook his head and followed Brock to the tiny spare room they used for medical emergencies and placed the woman on the bed. No sooner had he done that than he grabbed a sheet and draped it over her naked form.

"Thor, man, who is she? We can't just let some stranger in without asking Derrick and he's finally asleep with the triplets and Lucy—"

"Mine," Thor barked his answer, cutting off his Beta.

Oh fuck.

His Demon Wolf growled, smiling Wolfishly in his mind's eye. His shocked eyes met Brock's, and he realized the man was just as surprised as he was. Now that he said it aloud, he knew it was true.

"She's a Raven Shifter. She fell from the sky, and I caught her," Thor explained, running a hand over his face.

"What? Mates are just falling from the sky now?" Brock asked, scratching his head.

"She is not my mate," he argued, more for himself than Brock.

Oh yes she is, Demon Wolf argued back.

"Well, whoever she is, her arm looks broken. We need to call someone—"

"Me. No one else sees her. No one else touches her. I can set it," Thor replied, and somehow, he simply knew he could.

That was another thing about having *the sight*, Thor could sometimes glean information from the spirits. Right then, a healer ancestor was sending him instructions on how to feel for breaks and dislocation. Luckily, it was the latter.

Still, he knew it would hurt when he popped her shoulder back into place. Thor directed Brock on how to assist him. Though he hated the other male's hands on her.

Grrr.

Get the fuck over it, he told his Wolf.

Thor needed Brock's help. Jealousy was not a good look on him, and he would have to figure out how to handle the tidal wave of emotions hitting him and knocking him off balance. Thor pushed all that from his mind. He needed her all healed up so he could decide what to do about all this.

And he did not just mean the part of him screaming at him to mark, claim, and keep the woman. He also meant the undeniably possessive alphahole side of him that wanted to find whoever did this to her and remove that shit stain from the face of the earth.

"Dude, easy," Brock rumbled.

He realized he was still growling, even after the Beta had released her shoulders after Thor had re-set her arm. If the pain from that didn't wake her up, she would have been hurt more than he realized.

The thought did nothing to calm his beast, who was desperate to rip out of his skin. It was that fiercely loyal side of him that made him a good Enforcer, among other things. But even with the need for vengeance burning in his veins, his Demon

Wolf could not bring himself to leave her. Not until he knew she was out of harm's way.

Her eyes fluttered open just as he put some salve on one of the dozens of scratches across her flesh. Thor paused, unmoving, while caught in her line of sight. The blue of her eyes was clearer now, and something inside him warmed at the fact he'd helped.

"Thank you," she whispered.

Her eyes were still laced with exhaustion and pain, but there was something else, too. Maybe relief.

Too much pain. Never again.

"You don't have to thank me," he whispered.

Unable to help himself, he moved closer, reaching up to brush back her wild curls from her face carefully. He'd covered her with a sheet to protect her modesty. Her comfort was tantamount to everything right then.

"Thank you anyway," she whispered, wincing with the effort.

"It's no problem. But I need you to tell me who."

Thor was aware of Brock lingering in the periphery of his vision. The Beta looked on, concerned as the fragile woman moaned softly, shivering as her body pushed her to heal. Finally, her gaze focused back on him, and it was laced with such sorrow, Thor's heart damn near stopped altogether.

"Who did this to you?" he repeated, intent on her answer.

"My mate," she answered, right before her eyes rolled up.

She had passed out again, and it was a good thing. Thor's heart seized in his chest, unadulterated rage filled him.

Her mate? No!

She could not belong to another. She just couldn't. What kind of man would do this to his woman? What kind of cowardly sack of shit could hurt the one person he was to protect and cherish?

Mate? No. Fuck that.

She was his, dammit. How could the Fates be so cruel?

Mine, snarled his Demon Wolf just before the animal tore out of him.

CHAPTER 2

*T*hree weeks.

That was how long she'd been hiding out with the Dire Wolf MC in Blue Valley, a suburb in south Jersey. Three weeks. That was when Domenica Corvo, Nica to her friends, had plummeted to what she'd thought was her death from the sky. Only she did not die.

Nica didn't even hit the hard, black asphalt that had been getting closer and closer as she lurched into a panicked freefall when the last thread holding her wing in place came undone with an agonizing snap. Something had stopped her fall. No, not something, but someone.

She'd been saved. Caught in the arms of a hulking brute who should have scared the poop out of her. But there was always something a bit off when it came to Nica and her sense of self-preservation. As in, she simply didn't have any.

Instead of being frightened by the tattooed giant with the shaved head, she couldn't help but admire him. Even if only from afar. Sigh. Three weeks. That was how long since she'd first spied her savior. It was also how long he'd been avoiding her.

She wasn't beautiful like the other women in the Pack. She was short, curvy, and a bit of a tomboy, really, with her lack of finesse and fashion sense. Maybe he preferred tall, sophisticated blondes or something.

Gods knew that was not her. Disappointment filled her and regret whenever she thought of the type of woman who might attract Thor Ulger. But even if he hated her on sight, at the very least, she'd expected some questions about her situation and how she'd landed there.

But other than the Alpha couple, no one else had asked. So, she just hadn't bothered to tell anyone her story. Derrick and Lucy Rand were wonderful, easy to talk to, and sympathetic to her plight. They'd offered her sanctuary, and she took it.

What else could she do? Nica had nowhere to go. Plus, she was curious. She wanted to know more about the big, quiet man with the dozens of intricate tattoos covering his arms, chest, belly, and even his neck. He was not bald, as she'd first thought, but rather, he shaved his head with a long, sharp knife. She knew this because she'd walked in on him once in one of the several bathrooms in the Pack House.

It was more like a compound now that they'd added suites and wings to it, keeping in line with the oldish design out front, but affording the Pack some privacy by dividing the rooms up. She was staying in an unoccupied bedroom, but it was located in Thor's wing.

She'd been startled at first and offered to move to another room. But he'd canted his head in that animalistic way he had about him and replied with one word, one very important word.

Stay.

That was all he said. *Stay.* And Nica did. Of course, she didn't let it go to her head. Thor said very little in general, and his wing had three bedrooms and a bathroom. Clearly, there was enough space for her.

No, she didn't make it weird. Or at least, she tried not to. He couldn't be interested in someone like her, anyway. But sometimes, to her secret pleasure, she found his eyes on her. Oh yes, sometimes he seemed to track her movements with intense, dark eyes.

It flattered her when she caught his attention even for a minute. Thor was something else. Something other. The rest of the Pack treated him with a mixture of respect and awe, and it was easy to see why.

Part of her living with the Pack deal was that she would work to pay her way. Nica didn't mind at all, in fact, she loved working. As a Shifter, she had oodles of energy, and as a bird, well, she could get a bit flighty if that energy wasn't properly channeled.

So, yeah, working was a no brainer. And working at Serious Moonlight, the roadhouse she remembered hearing about from people in her old life, well, that was a thrill in and of itself. The place was renowned for their excellent dining, which she got to sample from world class chef, and Pack beta, Brock Laurent himself. The bands were phenomenal. And she had the best view whenever she worked at the front bar.

Sigh.

Nica's eyes darted across the room to where Thor sat, watching the door in his position as bouncer. He wore fitted jeans and a tight black t-shirt, his permanent scowl already in place. Boy, but he was fine. The man was enormous. Taller than the rest of the Pack, with huge cords of muscles roped around his body. She'd seen him without a shirt once and had dreamed about it for days after.

His shoulders were immense, pecs curved and hard, and his abs had abs before they tapered off to his trim waist. And yes, he even had that elusive V she'd read about in some of the racier novels she once borrowed from an online library. Still, for all his size and strength, Thor managed to not look bulky.

He looked perfect, *er*, well, he looked good. Just as she thought it, his black eyes flashed at her, and Nica squeaked, dropping the bowl of lemons she was currently slicing for drinks. Darn it. He always seemed to know when her thoughts started taking a naughtier turn than normal. But Nica couldn't help it. At least, not when it came to Thor.

Crud.

She really needed to find a better hobby than Thor-watching. She was becoming something of a stalker, she mused, shaking her head. Too bad the big, bad Wolf didn't seem to notice her at all. Derrick, the Alpha, couldn't have picked a better man for the job. His aura seemed to scream Enforcer, even if that secret part of her, her Raven side, who sometimes saw more than it should, whispered to her when no one else was around.

He's not just an Enforcer. He's much more. Mine.

Eek! Nope. She was not going there. Besides, it didn't matter what the bird thought. Thor Ulger might be one badassed motherhumper, strong, loyal, handsome as sin, especially with all that marvelous body art, but there was one more thing he was. And that was not interested in Nica Corvo.

Not in the least.

So yeah, she could admire his body, and his gorgeous and intricate tattoo work, but only from afar. Thor wanted nothing to do with her, obviously. When all was said and done, Nica would leave someday soon, and that would be that.

Speaking of tattoos, she wondered why his back was the only part of him that seemed free of ink. Maybe it was because he couldn't reach it. She'd learned from Sheila, the Alpha's cousin, that Thor was responsible for all the body art in the Pack, and the thought of that man as an artist stole her breath away.

Her favorite piece was a wreath of flames circling his thick neck. Fire had never looked so hot as it did on him. The man simply had too many muscles for one person. It was hardly necessary, for Pete's sake. But there it was.

There he was. Like some Greek, or in his case, Norse god, looking down on the rest of the mortals from his lofty perch, *er*, barstool. Muscles rippling with every move, he seemed oblivious to all the female eyes coveting him, and Nica felt her jealousy rise in response.

Sighing, she went back to cutting lemons after having retrieved them from the bar top. She had no business feeling possessive about the man. Thor wasn't hers.

"Take a picture, honey. It lasts longer," Sheila said, surprising her.

She winked as she wiped down the bar where Nica was supposed to be working, slicing lemons, and filling the condiment trays. Her cheeks burned at being caught staring. She was just glad the pretty she-Wolf could not read her train of thought.

Nica would have sounded like a crazed female in heat, the way she was panting after the man who clearly was not interested. Besides, there was no reason for this other than maybe some misplaced hero worship.

Raven Shifters did not experience a heat cycle. Not like Felines or Canines did. Bad enough she'd fallen from the sky to land in his lap, literally. The last thing she needed to do was walk around, giving him puppy eyes.

But it was more than that, even she was not ready to admit it aloud. Thor was the first male she had ever really felt connected to. Her Raven croaked, the deep guttural sound making her animal's preference for the male known.

CHAPTER 3

The music got louder as the band switched from a power ballad to something faster, so folks could dance. Nica tapped her foot and shrugged, slightly embarrassed at being caught by her peer.

"I wasn't staring exactly," Nica mumbled, but Sheila just gave her a look.

"Yeah, right, but Nica, you can look all you want. Still, you should know that Demon Wolf right there is not like the others. Thor is deep. He's got power and a temper, too," Sheila informed her.

"Demon Wolf? Like he's evil or something?" Nica asked, confused.

"Hell, no, girl. He ain't evil," the redheaded she-Wolf continued. "Thor is touched by the gods. He's our Seer. That means he has the sight. You know, ancient Vikings didn't use the term Demon like Christians do. You see, Demons were simply other-worldly beings. Folks like Thor, who have a foot on either side of the veil."

"I knew he was special, but I had no idea," Nica mused aloud, wonder lacing her tone.

"Yep. That Demon Wolf is pretty special. Look at those shoulders and thighs. No doubt about it, the man is *s-p-e-c-i-a-l*," she spelled it out, thrusting her hips with each letter.

Nica rolled her eyes and laughed at Sheila, who giggled, and play bumped her on the shoulder. It was strange, but she felt a sort of camaraderie with the Dire Wolves she'd never felt with anyone back home.

No, not home, Nica corrected herself.

The place she'd been kept for close to six years had never been her home. She shivered, wishing things were different, wishing she were different. Her gaze wandered back to where Thor was checking the IDs of a group of young women, all giggling and pretty.

The females looked happy and free, confident with their tight clothes and made-up faces. Just out for a good time, she supposed. Nica could not help envying their easy looking lives. One even dared to flirt with the unusually large and somber male. Thor's black gaze was on the blonde as she leaned in and spoke to him, her eyes smiling in invitation.

Something ugly and dark twisted in Nica's gut, and she frowned, recognizing that feeling for what it was. Jealousy. But she had no cause for that. She didn't have any claim on the stoic Dire Wolf Shifter. Behaving the fool was something she couldn't afford nowadays. Nica had other worries, serious worries, but she couldn't help but watch as he dealt with the trio of blonde beauties.

All three of them had the same golden stare and lithe physiques. They moved with a grace she identified as belonging to Feline Shifters only. Lionesses, if she had to guess. Serious Moonlight, the Dire Wolf MC's roadhouse and bar, was located right on the border of Blue Valley, prime Pride territory.

They wore skintight jeans and crop tops with strips of tanned skin revealed through expertly cut rips in their clothing. Yeah, they looked good. Confident, too. Perky boobs and tight butts were on display, with their tiny little waists showing off belly button rings and chains.

Nica felt downright dowdy by comparison. She was short and leaning towards the chubby side, despite being a Raven Shifter. Where her animal form was fine-boned and capable of flying, her human body was thick and stocky, with more soft curves than sleek muscles.

She had dark brown curly hair that she usually pulled back into an untamed puff on top of her head. Unless she had hundreds of dollars to spend on conditioning treatments, which she did not, the frizz was a constant in her life. Then there was her face. She had smooth skin, clear of blemishes save for a few freckles on her nose.

But Nica was allergic to most makeup, so she never bothered with the stuff. Her eyes were nice. A bright, clear blue that was attractive, if not pretty. Still, Nica was the kind of girl who'd rather stay home in yoga pants and a t-shirt watching reruns of old sitcoms and eating ice cream out of the carton than get dressed up and go bar hopping.

Yep. That settled it. Nica would never attract a man like Thor. Still, she watched him as he handled the randy Lionesses without moving off his barstool. He was smooth and professional, allowing them entry but not entertaining any of their flirtations. The leader seemed determined. Bold, that one was, for sure.

Thor mostly ignored the female, and for some reason, that made Nica feel better. Her Raven croaked again, a rumbling sound that showed her animal's content. At least the Demon Wolf, as Sheila had dubbed him, was as indifferent to the pretty Lioness group as he was to Nica.

She recalled how he'd reacted when, to her undying shame, Nica had sought him out after she'd recovered. Her healing sleep had lasted for nearly thirty-six hours after she'd fled her former Murder. Of course, her flight was on the heels of the Crow King's cruel punishment that had left her naked and bleeding, tied to a post outside like an animal.

No. Not mine. They were never my Murder.

In the wild, a group of ravens was called an *unkindness*, but even then, they were rare. Ravens tended to live solitary lives, sometimes in pairs, but only that. There were so few Ravens, they often flocked to other Flight Shifters who were more common. Like Crows.

A group of Crow Shifters was called a Murder, and aptly so. The last one she belonged to held just about as much warmth as the word itself. Harsh and cold, the Crow king was a liar, but duty kept his good little soldiers in line, and no one had helped Nica while the male had beat on her. Some had joined in under his orders.

That memory was forever burned into her brain,

destroying any kind thoughts she might have ever had about the Pine Murder. After Nica had finally woken from her healing sleep, she'd been full of sweet thoughts and gratitude towards the man who literally caught her before she could crash land on the unforgiving asphalt.

Thor was her savior, and she had to tell him how grateful she was. So, Nica had cornered him that very afternoon, gushing with emotion when she tried to thank him. His reply to her thankful praise echoed in her ears, and embarrassment filled her once more.

"Stop saying thank you. It's done."

No doubt about it. Thor Ulger was no fan of hers. He was ice. Frozen through to the bone, that one. Just a statue where a warm, breathing man should be, and she would do well to leave him alone. Some men were just like that. Cold, unfeeling brutes, incapable of affection and unwilling to form lasting relationships.

More memories swarmed inside her mind, sending shivers through her body. She'd learned her lesson about men the hard way. The first time she'd seen Jack Branwen, King of the Pine Murder, Nica was barely twenty years old. Green and gullible, she'd believed the older male when he told her he was in love with her and wanted to make her his queen.

Her widowed mother had been thrilled at the news and could not wait to ship her off. After a brief ceremony, Nica and Jack promised themselves to each other beneath a blooming cherry tree with his Beta, Emmet, and her mother as witnesses.

Oh, he'd been sweet then. Paying her compliments, the first she'd ever gotten from a man. Jack was never handsome, but he was so commanding, with his sharp features and fathomless eyes. He'd read her poetry, brought her roses and sweet cakes from the market near the place where she'd grown up in Maryland.

Jack was tall and lean, his face too hawklike to be truly handsome with his large nose and long black hair. He looked like something out of a Vampire romance. But he was no Vampire, he was a Crow. A King to his people. And Nica was so lucky he chose her. Wasn't that what her mother said?

"You should be grateful, child, looking the way you do. Too fat to land a regular man, but he sees value in those wide hips of yours," she snapped when Nica had hesitated about accepting his proposal. *"You will not get a better offer!"*

So, Nica accepted him at face value. She allowed

him to court her, took his gifts, and believed his lies when he said he loved her and wanted her. She hadn't questioned a thing.

What a foolish girl I'd been. I deserved what happened.

She shook her head, wiping a tear that escaped her eye before anyone could see it. Jack had done a real number on Nica. He loved playing his little games, making her apologize for things she didn't even know she did wrong, and always making it feel like it was her fault when they disagreed or when she had a difference of opinion.

It was never about anything important until he wanted more than the chaste kisses she offered him whenever they returned from a date.

"I'm a man, Nica, not a boy. I need more from you."

"I'm sorry, Jack. I don't know how—I'm a virgin," she'd confessed one night, guiltily.

"I see. You want a contract first. Fine, I'll meet with your mother tomorrow.".

True, they hadn't done more than kiss, but she didn't know what he meant by contract until her mother explained she was Jack's the next night. Then she told Nica to wear her one good Sunday dress, and she drove her to the cherry tree where Ravens had been making their intentions known for years and years. Nica had heard stories about the promising ceremony, but she never expected to have one for herself.

Fear and excitement warred within her, but the sharp look on her mother's face was as much incentive as the idea of finally getting out of her small hometown and the house she was raised in. Nica's mother was never affectionate with her, and she wanted more from life than waiting tables.

Jack's offer seemed too good to be true, but she wouldn't learn about that till much later. After she'd signed the papers he'd thrust at her, and they spoke their promise to mate one another aloud as per the ceremony, Jack drove Nica to a cheap motel where he took her virginity with Emmet waiting outside the door—what a horrible disappointment that night was. Eye opening, too.

Sex was painful and messy, and over too damn quickly for her to do more than wince and gasp. Jack was angry at the way she'd received him, her lack of warmth. But she was a virgin, and he didn't seem to care.

"Christ, that was rough. Let's fuck off back to the trailer park. Maybe Ella and Denise can teach this little puritan something about sex before I have to bed her again."

Oh, yeah. She'd heard every scathing thing he'd

growled about her to Emmet while she'd been in the bathroom, using a damp washcloth to clean the blood from between her legs and soothe the hurt he'd left there. When she was finished, he demanded she get in the car, then Jack and Emmet drove her to the trailer park where he and the others in his Murder lived.

Nica was almost relieved when he put her inside a trailer with two other females and told she would have to wait her turn to marry the King. She didn't understand, but when she questioned him, Jack told her the promise ceremony they'd had in front of her mother was just that, a promise to marry in the future.

"You ain't the only one in line. Let's see if you can hold my seed better than the others," Jack said, nodding at her stomach.

Nica felt as if the floor had dropped out from under her. Not growing up in a Murder, she did not understand the politics. Apparently, Jack wanted her pregnant before he mated her. That was news to her. Nica wanted to finish school and maybe spend some time getting to know him first.

Thank goodness Ella and Denise had been kind upon her arrival. Ella was ten years older than Nica, with blonde hair and a tall, willowy frame. She was a

Crow Shifter who had been promised to Jack since they were teenagers.

Denise was shorter than Ella, but still taller than Nica, with bronzed skin and sharp features and straight black hair. She had been brought in about two years before Nica. The Crow King was apparently desperate for an heir, and after failing to get either of them pregnant, he was still looking for a fertile female to be his Queen.

Lucky for Nica, she had started birth control back in high school to help regulate her period. Still, her reality had hit her hard. She was no treasured mate and there was no impending marriage.

Jack Branwen was a liar.

What she'd thought was the happiest time in her life turned out to be the worst. She was the third in line to mate the Crow King, and she paid her way by cleaning and cooking, doing laundry and other housework the females were told to do. She was made to quit her classes and all outside activity. Her life was to be dedicated to the Murder.

Funny thing was, pathetic as it might sound, Nica could have handled that. She would have done the dishes and washed the clothes, hell, she would have scrubbed the windows and the floors till her fingers bled, if only he loved her. But Jack never loved her. It didn't take her long to realize that. Unfortunately, there was a reason a group of Birds like them was called a Murder—*death was the only way to leave.*

Unlucky at love. That's what you are, Nica girl. Terribly unlucky.

CHAPTER 4

"Nica? A Word," Derrick poked his head out of his office and called out to her from down the hall.

She turned her head, placing the last of the lemon slices in the condiment tray. Raven Shifters might have an inferior sense of smell when it came to other Shifters, but her hearing was just fine. And her sight, well, that was even better.

She placed the clear plastic cover back on the tiny tray, taking a second to enjoy the rainbow of sliced lemons, oranges, limes, cherries, and such, before she wiped her hands and headed to Derrick's office.

"Yeah, boss?" she asked, knocking before entering.

"Sit down, Nica," he invited, patting the back of the baby he held.

Nica smiled. The triplets were the most beautiful babies she had ever seen. At almost one month old, they were triple the size of a human baby, and alert in the way of Shifter offspring. She was delighted with the way the entire Pack pitched in to take care of the cubs. It wasn't something she was used to growing up with just her mother.

Catherine Corvo was the opposite of what Nica thought of when it came to maternal instincts. Her mother saw to the necessities like keeping food on the table and a roof over her head, but she never witnessed the kind of utter joy she saw on the faces of Lucy and Derrick when they held their precious young. If only she should be so lucky someday, she mused, laughing as the baby let out a surprisingly loud burp.

"That's my girl," Derrick murmured, grinning as he kissed her head.

"She's just perfect, Alpha Derrick," Nica said, smiling at the infant.

All three cubs were perfect, in her opinion. Their cherubic faces were as pretty as their names—*Eden, Astrid,* and *Selena.* Nica watched the new father as he gently placed the now sleeping babe in a bassinet, just in time to retrieve another, who was already fussing, as if she knew her sister was settled, and her daddy's hands were free just to tend her.

"Lucy is napping," he explained and nodded his head to a door where the Alpha couple had set up a mini nursery, complete with a rocking recliner and a daybed.

Nica smiled and reminded herself to speak softly so as not to wake the exhausted she-Cat. That was another thing she found interesting about this pack. They accepted everyone into the fold without issue. These Dire Wolves were mated to various Shifters and supes, even normals with no protests from the rest of the Pack. That was not something that would ever happen in the Pine Murder. Bad enough she'd been a Raven among Crows. After she'd refused to mate Jack, her status had dropped so low she'd been little more than a servant for years.

"You've been with us three weeks now—"

Oh, no!

Fear gripped her, and her stomach clenched. She should have seen this coming. Derrick stopped speaking to rearrange the baby's bib as he patted her back and burped her. But Nica was too nervous to be entertained by the homey scene now.

"I am so sorry if I'm wearing out my welcome,

Alpha," she began. "I swear, I will leave as soon as I have enough saved, but if you can see your way to giving me some more time."

She did not know how she would find the means to move on, but Nica was determined to not be a detriment to those who had helped her.

"Do you want to leave?" he asked suddenly, and Nica ducked her head.

She could not lie to the man, after all, he would smell it on her. But she was embarrassed by how much she actually wanted to stay. Her feelings were a mess lately, and part of that was due to the broken bonds she had with Jack and his Murder. She had to find some way to get rid of the remnants, so they couldn't find her before she even thought about leaving.

"No. I don't want to go," she said. "But I don't want to put you or your mate and cubs, the whole Pack, in any danger, either."

"Danger?"

"Well, so far, Jack and the Murder have stayed away, but there is no guarantee he will keep his distance, is there?"

"Do you know something you aren't telling me?" Derrick asked, eyes narrowed.

Nica swallowed. She knew Jack and his men

were out there watching, just waiting for the right time to strike. That's what Crows, and sometimes Ravens, did. They were the best spies, inconspicuous and seemingly harmless. But Nica knew better than that. She suspected they'd been scoping her out these last few weeks, and her blood chilled at the thought.

"Not for sure, but I, I think they might be watching me here," she whispered, ashamed of herself.

"I see," Derrick replied.

Nica was a coward for hiding behind these Dire Wolves. She despised that side of her that was just too weak to run. Isn't that what Jack had said about her all those years ago? She was too small, too meek, too fragile to make it on her own. So what that he had other women? Her feminine sensibilities had been affronted by his assumption she would simply obey his decrees.

After that first time in the motel, and once she'd known about his other mates, Nica refused his attentions. Oh, he punished her for it in different ways., but her resolve was rock solid. Sometimes his punishments were as simple as withholding food for the night or access to the trailer park's communal showers. But it got worse.

After six months of polite refusals, she was

forced to leave the trailer where Jack's other mates lived. No longer under that protected status, he'd reduced her rank and shoved her in a rundown shack instead.

She shivered, remembering the cold winters and sweltering summers in that four by six hovel. It was used to house lawn care equipment back when whoever had run the trailer park took care of things like that. By the time the Murder moved in, there was no grass to speak of.

Just a dusty lot with a smattering of trees surrounding it and the loud highway beyond an ugly, tall, brown wall that served as a noise barrier for the community. The stink of oil and gasoline had permeated the walls, but it didn't matter. Nica was spared Jack's drunken advances for a good long run as she cowered and hid behind her duties and her rank at the bottom of the Murder.

It wasn't until Ella got sick that it all started again. She frowned, thinking of the frail female who was the only one in the Murder who had maintained a friendly smile whenever she saw Nica hurry by. She hoped Ella was all right, prayed that Jack got her some medical attention, though it was unlikely.

Once his first mate fell ill, he'd tried courting her again, giving her extra rations at mealtimes, and sending her flowers. He'd just finished moving her stuff out of the shack and into a nicer, newer trailer one afternoon after washing the Murder's clothes at the local laundromat.

Nica was suspicious, nervous even. The man did nothing for anyone, not without a reason. She soon found out what he wanted that night when he let himself into her small bedroom, naked and stinking of booze. Nica had fought him like a wildcat, scratching and clawing anywhere she could reach.

That was the first night she'd tried to run, but Jack was so fast and strong. He'd caught her, beaten her, and let his Murder take turns attacking in their bird forms. Oh, they were just toying with her. They could have easily killed her, but he wanted her broken, not dead.

One of his soldiers had unwittingly cut the binds tying her to the pole Jack used to bind whoever was being punished. Nica hid the torn tethers until they gave up on her torture for the evening or just plain passed out. Once they were gone, she did not hesitate. She broke free and wound up here with the Dire Wolves.

For the first time, Nica had felt a spark of hope ignite inside her chest. She'd found a place she felt safe, wanted. Still, she would leave if Derrick told her to. She would have no choice.

"I am sorry I didn't say anything sooner," she fretted.

"Don't be sorry. Look, I am not chasing you away, Nica. You let me and the Pack worry about the Murder."

"Do you mean that?" she asked, surprised.

"Hell yeah," he whispered, the baby in his arms stirring slightly. "Truth is, we are so lucky you came to us when you did. With the cubs arriving early, and Lucy's replacement at the bar, Gwendolyn, still learning to control her new Wolf, your help here has been a godsend! I know it's unconventional, but I'd like you to seriously consider staying on with us as long as you want," Derrick said, surprising Nica into smiling.

"Well, all right then," she replied. "As long as you need me, I'll stay."

CHAPTER 5

"*W*ell, *all right then. As long as you need me, I'll stay.*"

Thor released the breath he was holding, and his entire body seemed to relax after hearing Nica's reply to Derrick's statement about needing her. Recently, he'd started to suspect she was growing restless. He had tracked her with hungry eyes. Saw the way she started watching the trees and the skies when she thought no one was looking.

Oh yeah, Thor had been clocking the curvy little Raven as she went about her business, picking up slack at the roadhouse and even taking on extra chores at the Pack House. How many times had the tiny female done laundry that wasn't hers? Or washed up after dinner when it wasn't her turn?

The other females made damn sure the men in the house knew they were not there to wait on them, but Nica seemed cut from a different cloth. She took on chores without complaint, so much so, he intervened when he thought others were taking advantage. Like when he caught her cleaning Cole's bedroom. He'd put a stop to that shit real fast, reminding her the single male was perfectly capable of washing his own bedding.

He'd also had a one-on-one conversation with Cole, which ended with the man wholeheartedly agreeing to never take advantage of Nica's kindness again. Thor didn't even have to say anything. He'd just tossed the pile of wet sheets he'd taken from Nica, she was about to hang them to dry on the outdoor line, right onto Cole's lap, followed by a single punch to the male's jaw.

But aside from throwing herself into her chores, Thor noticed something else strange about Nica. Not once in the three weeks that had passed had she shifted into her animal. But maybe it was odd to him because his own Demon Wolf had been acting like a total fucking lunatic.

Thor was so amped up with her around, he was shifting into his beast nightly. It was the only way to contain the animal's anger, lest he hunt down and decimate the first Murder he came across. Thank fuck she was a Shifter, and those bruises she'd arrived with were long gone by now. That was enough to placate his beast. Mostly.

Not a day went by that Thor didn't have a flashback of her broken wing, cuts oozing blood, and the black eye that had swollen so much by the time she woke up, she could hardly open it. Those first few days had been hell on him, and yeah, he realized he was whining like a cub, but fuck. He couldn't really explain it save to say it hurt him to see her hurt.

Thor's blood boiled with the thirst for revenge. He hungered for it. But revenge was not his to take. Finding her at last, Thor had given everything he could to help fix her battered body. He couldn't bring himself to leave her side, at least not till she told him the only thing that could have moved him.

Nica had a mate.

A right bastard for sure, but still her mate. The beautiful Raven was not free for Thor to claim. She just wasn't. Knowing it made his heart feel like someone had tried to rip it right out of his chest.

So, he'd done what any besotted fool, who had no chance in hell of claiming the woman the Fates told him was his, would do. He'd stayed away. Hid in the background. Watched from afar. And he cursed those same Fates for showing him something he couldn't have.

Why did she have to be so perfect? With her dark curls and bright blue eyes, and her fresh baked bread and sweet summer jam scent.

"You should talk to her, man," Weylin said, suddenly beside him.

The younger Wolf had been walking by, carrying a couple of cases of beer up from storage, but Thor hadn't been paying attention. He hadn't realized Weylin stopped beside him until the man opened his fat mouth with his Captain Obvious observations.

Gods dammit.

Could he really blame him, though? Weylin was still in that honeymoon phase with Gwendolyn, his somehow newly turned Dire Wolf mate. Newly matched up and just about as annoying as every other mated pair in the Pack, Thor could give two shits what Weylin thought.

"Don't go getting all growly and shit, all I'm saying is instead of stalking her like some giant psycho, you might try talking to the woman—hey!"

Thor tried to make it a point to hate as few things as possible in his life, but there were a few he just could not help but loathe. One of them was unsolicited advice. However, staring down at the mess he'd made of Weylin's perfectly coiffed red hair after dumping the glass of water he'd been holding was extremely satisfying.

In fact, Thor felt better than he had in days. Of course, that was probably because of his eavesdropping ways and overhearing Nica tell Derrick she was planning on staying for a while.

Good. Mine. Mate.

No. She belongs to another.

Grrrrrr.

Fine. Maybe Weylin had a point. Gifted, or cursed, with the sight as he was, Thor knew better than to just toss away something the Fates had so purposely thrown at him. He didn't pretend to understand the motives of supernatural deities and power players, but he knew enough that the shit they did was for a reason.

If Nica had fallen into his lap, so to speak, it was likely because he had a hand in her future. Thor wasn't the type of man to mess around with another male's mate, but perhaps that was the part he had wrong. Fact was, he needed answers, and he could only get them from her. So, yeah, maybe he should try talking to her. He grunted and nodded at the still sputtering Weylin. His advice was unsolicited, but useful.

Hmm. Imagine that.

Thor placed the empty water glass on top of the cases of beer his drenched Pack mate was still holding and walked away to mull things over. Perhaps he'd commune with the spirits tonight, see if they had any advice for him. It wasn't his favorite pastime, and it took fuck all out of him, but he needed to proceed with caution.

Could be he was mistaken, and Nica wasn't his fated mate, after all. But judging from the way his cock turned to steel behind the tight denim jeans he often wore every time he saw her, he doubted he erred in his assessment. As if to emphasize the fact his cock also disagreed, the damn thing thumped inside his jeans, filling with lust at the mere mention of her.

Yep. He really fucking doubted he was wrong. He needed to bide his time until she had a spare moment. So, Thor kept busy most of the night, working the front door, just business as usual. He didn't mind checking IDs and making sure the supernatural members of the mixed crowd Serious Moonlight attracted knew he was there to keep the peace. As the Pack Enforcer, it came with the territory.

Dire Wolves had a reputation for being tough,

and sometimes folks liked to challenge them just on the off chance they might win a fight. Not that it happened very often. Still, his senses were on high alert, the Demon Wolf inside him riled for whatever reason.

More than likely it had to do with the fact that Sheila, his redheaded Pack mate, and his Alpha's cousin, was teaching Nica how to tend bar. Sheila was mated and devoted to her man, but she could flirt with the best of them. Still, she was a spitfire and could hold her own where Nica was shy around most men.

He was concerned Sheila was going to push her outside her comfort zone, so he waited, poised to intervene. But he shouldn't have worried. Nica was holding her own. Pride, the likes of which he never felt for anyone, sprung inside him like a well.

Go on, girl. Show 'em how it's done, his Demon Wolf growled.

The curvy little goddess was grinning and pulling beers on tap with almost zero foam to the praise of their patrons. She was wearing a pair of skintight jeans strategically cut to show tantalizing swatches of smooth, unmarred skin. On top, Nica wore one of Serious Moonlight's famous logo tees, the deep V revealing her fantastic cleavage, making Thor's mouth water, and drawing the eyes of the male customers at the bar.

Grrrr.

It was part of the deal with bartending, but those guys could fuck right off if they wanted to keep their eyes inside their heads. They served mostly Shifters, so when one male leaned over, checking out her ass as he bent over to grab something from the cooler behind the bar, Thor sent a snarl his way. The young male blanched, sat his ass back down and treated Nica like she was his Sunday school teacher after that.

Good, but let's bite him, anyway, growled his Wolf.

But Thor knew better than to throw his weight around. Saying he was a big man was like saying Texas was a big state—at the very least, it was a bland way of describing something that sizeable. The Lone Star state was the second largest state in the country after Alaska. It was fucking vast.

In the same sense, Thor was not simply *big*. He was the biggest motherfucker in the bar, including a couple of Grizzly Shifters and that fat-headed Lion mate of Sheila's. Leo was okay, but what was with that fucking hair? The man used more conditioner than all of Thor's sisters combined, and he'd grown up with three. They were all spread out now across the world, mothers, the lot of them, and happy as little mated clams. But he'd still bet Leo used more hair product than any of them.

It had been a while since he'd checked in on them, and he made a mental note to do that. The line outside was growing, and he calculated the numbers before allowing the next group in. There were legal limits to how many they could have under their roof at one time, and Thor was highly conscientious of that.

He growled at a group of underage Bears, turning the rascals away by pulling his top lip away from his teeth, revealing enormous fangs. Those cubs couldn't run away fast enough. The next trio were of age, and female, even better for the bar. It might be sexist, but it was the business. Women brought in men, which added up to a packed house, and that added up to paying customers. Sure, their money was mostly made on the market, and gods knew, the Pack had plenty. But there was something about making Serious Moonlight a success that meant a lot to each of them.

Thor didn't think it would happen, but Derrick had been right about all this. Settling down, growing roots, making a home. Thor had to agree. For the first time, he found contentment in a patch of land.

Blue Valley was turning out to be ideal. Now if only he could have a conversation with a certain curly haired beauty, then maybe, just maybe, his Demon Wolf would be okay, too.

Tonight's band was thumping, some local Wolves singing country rock with a little hip hop thrown in. They were pretty good, but he just wasn't paying enough attention to really judge. There was a sizeable group of normals amongst the crowd of mostly Shifters, but they were all right, too, seeming to just want to have a good time.

Thor kept an eye on everyone. It was his job, but there was more to it than that. As a Seer, he picked up on auras and inklings, things the Spirits were trying to tell him, messages, and warnings. It was like he was always on, constantly reading from ten different books, in ten different languages. He had to pay attention not to lose track of one or the other.

It was a unique dance he did, keeping steady, maintaining balance. Keeping watch over the Pack and those who meant the most to him was a most sacred duty. For years, he assumed that was why he was not mated. How could he focus on one and the other at the same time? It worried him, even now.

When he wasn't watching Nica, of course. She was so damn pretty. Far as he could tell, she didn't seem to know it. Her heart-shaped face was free of makeup, save a little lip gloss. He never really liked artificial things, and Nica was anything but fake. She was more beautiful than anyone he had ever seen.

Thor was a spiritual guy, and he wasn't all that fond of fake things and materialism. Didn't matter to him if a person lived in a mansion or a cardboard box, he made up his mind about someone based on how they acted. So far, Nica had been sweet and kind, patient, and hardworking. She was a good one. He could tell.

Suddenly, her head snapped towards him, and Thor froze, thinking he'd been caught staring. But she wasn't looking at him. Her gaze was fixed beyond where he stood a few feet away from the front door and his usual barstool perch. Her face blanched, and those blue eyes he'd been obsessing over widened with fear. That's when he smelled them.

Feathers.

Thor turned and spotted them immediately. Six tall, thin Shifters, Crows he was betting, walked into the bar, fanning out and taking up way too much space as far as he was concerned. His Demon Wolf snarled deep inside the metaphysical plane where the beast waited to be called.

Enemies, the animal growled.

Yes, Thor agreed.

Animosity and anger seemed to roll off the males in waves, but it would take a fucking tsunami to knock Thor off his substantial feet. The one in front looked the most dangerous. That had to be the Crow King, Thor assumed. He had a broody expression, muddy eyes, long black hair, and a big nose.

Good. Easy to break, the Demon Wolf inside him snarled.

They advanced, but Thor stopped them, positioning himself in front of the leader. One of the lackeys held their IDs, but Thor did not give two shits about that. He ignored him, focusing on the so-called King. Thor's Pack bonds lit up, and he felt his Pack mates easing next to him, Cole on his left, and Weylin on his right.

"Pardon us, friend." The man smiled, but it did not reach his eyes.

"No." Thor said. His voice had been clear, so he was mildly confused when the fella replied.

"Excuse me?"

"I said, no. You are not welcome here, Crow. Leave. Now."

"Show him some respect," one of the lackeys said, stepping forward.

All Thor had to do was flick his gaze in the male's direction to stop him in his tracks. That laser like focus, and his uncanny ability to see into the minds and hearts of people, was often enough to halt whatever tomfoolery was about to happen. Thor was used to leaving folks shaky and vulnerable when he gazed upon them with the *sight*.

"Fuck. Off." Thor growled.

This Murder was tainted. He knew it. They knew it, too. But they were too scared or too lazy to do anything about it. Unfortunately for them, that was not Thor's problem. The Crows would have to work out their issues themselves. But not here. Not anywhere near Nica.

"Gentlemen, calm yourselves. Our Wolf friends require an introduction," he explained and raised his hands in a fake gesture of peace. "I am Jack Branwen, King of the Pine Murder. And I demand to speak with your Alpha about returning something he has of mine," the Crow King sneered.

"There is nothing for you here, Crow. And you are most decidedly unwelcome," Thor grunted, unfolding his arms.

His chest was heaving and the growl in his chest grew louder with every passing moment. Before he could advance on the hawkish King and his smarmy grin, Cole got in front of him. The gray-eyed Dire Wolf opened his arms, hands spread and nodded to the door.

"Look, tonight we have *mixed company*," Cole explained, his intention clear. There were humans in the bar. It was not an ideal time for a fight.

"However, if you would like to arrange a meeting for a later date? Who has a card? No one? No matter. Here is mine," he said, handing a business card to one of the Crows standing beside the King. "I suggest you leave now and call tomorrow after ten."

A few more minutes of the Crow King trying to stare Thore down resulted in nothing but frustration for the man with the big nose. Thor could have kept that shit up all fucking day. He even knew the second his eyes bled to black by the way the man startled. The Crow even swallowed a loud gulp full of fear.

Grrrr.

That was a foolish thing to do in front of a predator. Thor pulled on his powers, calling on the Spirits to delve into the man's mind and heart. Likely, the Crow King did not realize what Thor was, never mind how much he wanted to end him. Blackness and evil intent came back at him, and the Demon

Wolf snarled again. The Crow King did not just want Nica. He wanted to break her.

Fuck. No. That was so not going to happen. Thor refused to look away, even when the Crow broke eye contact.

"Fine. Tomorrow," clipped Jack Branwen.

Then he left with his men, and Thor closed his eyes, trying to rein in his beast. It wasn't easy when all he wanted to do was follow him outside and tear the piece of shit limb from limb. Derrick would not approve. But as far as the Demon Wolf was concerned, Jack Branwen's number was up. It was merely a matter of when.

Grrrr.

CHAPTER 6

*D*amn. *Damn. DAMN.*

Nica waited until after the bar was closed to have her first freak out in the weeks since she'd come to be there. She'd been on edge ever since she escaped Jack's clutches and despite Derrick's assurances the Pack could handle a bunch of Crows, she didn't want to bring that kind of heat down on them.

Crows fought dirty, and the Dire Wolves were just so different from the other predatory Shifters she'd been around. They were loyal and honorable. They seemed to have the deepest respect for community and family, and well, Nica just didn't know what to do with that. How did you show gratitude for something you never even knew was a possibility?

After the Murder appeared in the bar, she expected the shit to hit the fan, and for the Alpha to rescind his invitation. But that didn't happen. In fact, no one said a word to her. She'd watched as the guys filed into Derrick's office after that tense little meet and greet. Nica even stayed close, waiting to be called in. But she wasn't.

If this situation were reversed, and she'd brought trouble to the Murder, Jack would have had her tied to that horrible post in the trailer park and beaten in front of everyone. That was his go to form of punishment. He'd done it to others, and he did it to her after the countless nights of her refusing his advances.

"Nica, what was all that about?" Sheila asked, sliding up next to her. "Look, I know we haven't really talked about your past, but that was pretty intense."

"Crud. I am sorry, Sheila. Derrick and Lucy know everything, but I just didn't think anyone else cared—"

"Oh, honey, no! We care. We were just waiting for you to open up."

"Really?" Nica was shocked, but it was time for a break anyway, and Sheila dragged her over to a small table where she had some appetizers waiting.

"Come on, spill," the redheaded firebrand said.

Ariella, Tracey, and Gwen were there, too. All the women looked concerned, and like they wanted to help. Tears pricked Nica's eyes, and before she knew it, she'd spilled. Like *everything*.

"Look, no matter how much you liked or felt sorry for those two women, Ella and Denise, you were right to refuse to become like them," Tracey remarked, her brows furrowed in anger, but not at Nica.

"They're just Jack's possessions," Gwen added, but she was more upset than she was judging them, Nica could tell.

"Ella was sick when I got away. I feel bad, like I abandoned them," she confessed.

"No, that is not on you. You had to do what you needed to survive," Ariella replied, her hand on Nica's arm, reassuring her. "I don't know anything about the way Murders are run, but my sisters and I would have torn those Crow males limb from limb. I am glad you got away, Nica, no matter how you did it." The Lioness nodded, and the others seemed to agree.

"Oh my, thank you all so much. I mean, I never had a lot of friends growing up, but I always imag-ined what it would be like, and you ladies are blowing it out of the water," she said, her cheeks burning with embarrassment.

"Hell, honey, we like you too," Sheila replied, and Nica felt her own wobbly smile on her face in return.

"Are they dangerous, though?" Gwen asked, and Nica could not dishonor her new friends with a lie.

"Yes. Crows are dangerous, but not in the same way you and your mates are. Oh, they are plenty strong, but worse than brute strength is how they think. You see, Crows are wily, sneaky, and cruel. Very, very cruel," she replied and worried her lower lip.

They divvied up the last of the mozzarella sticks before break time was over. The next half hour went by quickly, and she mulled over what the Pack females had said. Maybe she was wrong to feel guilty. One thing she knew, this was like a second chance for her, and she was wasting it being idle. She had to speak to Thor.

Sooner than she knew it, closing time approached and Nica was wiping down the bar while most of the Pack males were still inside the Alpha's office. She moved on with her spray and rag, cleaning every available surface in the bar, and was just tying up the trash bag when she saw them leaving. Of course, her eyes zeroed in on him.

Thor Ulger came out of Derrick's office, oozing confidence, and barely muted fury. His face was normally a mask, hiding all of his emotions—assuming he had any. And tonight, that assumption was correct.

Nica gasped as he walked into the room. She could practically feel his rage, and it was stunning in its purity. His dark eyes flicked to hers for one poignant moment, and it was like he sucked all the air out of the room before he mercifully looked away.

She inhaled, hardly aware she was trembling till she looked down at the spray bottle in her hand. Forcing herself to be still, she placed it on the table nearest her. Music played low in the background, some hip-hop song one of the guys played while they cleaned up. But Nica couldn't name the song or the artist, how could she? When Thor walked into a room, the man simply commanded all of her attention. Every. Last. Bit of it. Like he was a superstar or politician or something.

There was never any opportunity to go to concerts or the big city, despite being so close. Not for Nica, anyway. But she imagined this was how she would have reacted to seeing one of her favorites up on stage or maybe in passing outside of some posh little café in the Village. Her reactions, of course, were grossly embarrassing.

Nica got tongue-tied and turned into a quivering mess whenever Thor was in the same room as her. Liquid pooled between her legs, and her nipples turned into pebbles. She didn't know why or how to stop it. All she knew was that when he was near, her stomach tensed, breathing grew erratic, and she felt hot all over, like her skin was too tight. Something sparked, and it spread through her veins like molten lava. Even her clothes irritated the hell out of her. It was sort of like when she needed to shift, but different.

Yes, different, her Raven pushed the thought at her, and she exhaled slowly.

Thor was gone. She didn't have to look up to know that for sure. Nica could tell he'd left by the ease with which she took her next breath. Of all the males in the Dire Wolf MC, Thor was the only one who made her chest feel tight and the baby hairs on the back of Nica's neck stand up whenever he was near. Her inner Raven watched him, always. But her animal had always been more curious than was good for her. Still, she knew what she saw, and she knew it was bad.

Jack had found her. The Crow King and his men had tracked her to Serious Moonlight. To Thor and his Pack. Damn it. It was time for her to run again. But she couldn't go yet, not without knowing what the evil man said to Thor about her.

Usually, her hearing was good enough that the distance wouldn't have mattered, but the bar had been crowded and their speech too low for her ears. Her Raven croaked deep and low, this time the sound was anything but content. Grabbing her courage, she rushed out the side door.

Determination filled her. She needed to track Thor to find out what happened before she took her next steps towards freedom from that horrible Crow. Only, she'd sort of forgotten the very real physical reactions she had when she was near him and rushed to the building where she sensed he'd gone.

"C-can I talk to you?" she asked, her voice barely above a whisper.

Nica should have put something on, a sweatshirt maybe, anything to cover herself up. She was highly aware of the low-cut t-shirt she'd worn to tend bar and the fact it revealed way more skin than she was used to showing off. But it was too late now. Nica shivered involuntarily, hovering by the open door of the enormous garage that sat on the other side of the parking lot across from the bar.

Actually, it was a barn the Pack had converted into their own personal garage. A place where they could work on the dozens of motorcycles they owned, and usually displayed in front of the road-house to attract other enthusiasts. It was nothing like the Murder's old trailer park or the shack where she'd spent so many nights in her bird form. Her stomach was all clenched up tight, and she wondered where she had finally found the nerve to approach him.

Meek, weak, small, insignificant thing. Who are you to bother him?

She closed her eyes to quiet those ugly voices inside her head. Jack and the Murder had loved to break down any female who dared speak out. Espe-cially the ones who turned down offers to share their beds. They'd called her stuck up and conceited, a cock tease who needed to be broken. They just couldn't even see the real problem was with them-selves. She shivered again, hating the idea of going back.

No. I won't go.

They'd have to kill her first, she vowed with renewed determination. Thor still hadn't looked up from what he was doing, but she'd seen him these past weeks and knew he would answer in his own time. The man simply would not be rushed.

That was okay. She could wait. Besides, she enjoyed looking around at all the bikes and parts. It sure didn't smell like any garage she had ever seen. Not that there had been many. To Nica, it looked like some sort of motorcycle museum.

Shelves were immaculately kept, row after row of parts new and refurbished, some still inboxes. They had powerful looking tools, dozens of them, each cleaned and put in its place. That was how every-thing was inside there. Everything was either new or clean, kept with the utmost care, and returned to its proper place. Everything but Nica.

Always the odd duck.

She bit her lip, waiting for him to acknowledge her. Finally, he turned to face her, and Nica damn near swallowed her tongue. She normally had to bend her neck back just to look at him, but not this time. She was about eye level with him almost kneeling on the floor.

Even that didn't stop her from feeling so small compared to him. Thor was crouched down, working on his enormous Harley. Nica had asked Cole about the makes and models one evening when she'd been hanging the wash on the outside line.

Before the Alpha fem had given birth to her triplets, she'd been obsessed with the scent of laundry freshly washed and hung outside to dry. Since Nica didn't mind the work, she'd kept it up for the weeks she'd stayed there.

Happy to help.

"What is it?" Thor clipped.

His deep, gravelly voice cut through her reverie and Nica startled, clutching her throat and he stood up swiftly, running a hand over his shaved head and cursing to himself.

"Fuckin hell," he muttered.

"You shouldn't cuss."

"I shouldn't cuss?" he asked, head canted to the side.

"Yeah, you shouldn't cuss."

"Is that why you came in here? To tell me not to cuss?" he asked, eyes wide with incredulity.

"What? No! Um, w-what did they say to you?" Nica asked, averting her gaze.

Staring into Thor's impossibly dark eyes was almost too much for Nica to bear. The tight black t-shirt he wore did nothing to hide the rippling muscles corded around his chest, arms, back, and abs. Same thing went for the well-worn denim clinging to his rugby player thighs.

He was a powerhouse of a man. The few times she'd seen him without a shirt had left her tongue-tied and aching in a way she hadn't felt since those days when she'd thought Jack Branwen was the sweetest thing in the world. Actually, that was not true.

This feeling eclipsed her first tastes of carnal hunger. But Nica knew better than to let it show. There was no way on earth a man like Thor Ulger would want anything to do with her. And that was what she'd been telling herself every day for the last three weeks.

Hide your feelings. Keep your heart safe.

"What did they say? They who?"

"Them, the, uh, the Crows," she murmured, hating even saying that out loud.

"You mean your mate," he growled the word and raw fury flashed in his black eyes.

Nica shook her head. Thor looked furious. His expression was thunderous as he slowly turned towards her. The muscles on his chest and abs flexed as he tried to control his breathing, but they were mesmerizing. Instead of being afraid as she should have been, Nica felt bold and curious, warm all over.

"You've got that wrong," she explained, and started towards him. "Jack's not my mate."

"You called him mate."

"When? Anyway, no, I mean, he was supposed to be, but h-he lied," she blurted, trying to catch up.

Thor went still, lifting a hand to halt her advance, and Nica fumbled. What the heck was she doing? Why was she so intent on getting closer to a man who could not stand her? Her Raven cawed, and she shook her head, trying to clear some of the fog.

"You said your mate hurt you. The day you fell," he grumbled.

"I did? Well, I mean, we were supposed to be mated, but he already had two mates when he brought me to the trailer park, and, um, I j-just couldn't," Nica replied, racking her brain for more of an explanation.

Thinking was hard with Thor staring daggers at her. Hell, the man must truly hate her to look like that, and the thought made her sad. He seemed to wait for more from her, but the truth was, she simply wasn't used to talking about herself. And after a couple of years of living as an outcast in the

Pine Murder, she was unaccustomed to talking period.

"I'm going to need you to explain what you mean by that, Nica. Start from the beginning."

Nica swallowed. A cool Autumn breeze swept in through the open door of the garage and she shivered involuntarily. Thor stood there, eyes glittering darkly despite the fluorescent overhead light. He wanted an explanation from her. But why? Curiosity got the better of her, and Nica couldn't have walked away now if she wanted to. And she didn't want to, she realized as the word he'd spoken to her the first night after she woke from her healing sleep echoed inside her head.

Stay.

CHAPTER 7

Fuck. *Fuck. FUCK.*

Thunder roared in Thor's brain, and he wanted to hit something just to make it stop. He was angry, furious at himself, at Derrick for ordering him weeks ago not to seek retaliation against those hateful fucking cowards who'd hurt her. Only an Alpha's order could have stopped him from going after the stain, who so richly deserved the vengeance Thor wanted to reap against him.

Should've hit that prick. Should've given him a nice shiner like he gave our Nica, his Demon Wolf snarled.

Thor expelled a harsh breath, the growl in his chest never ending as he tried to control his emotions. The second that Crow motherfucker had left the bar with his lackeys, Thor had to use all his strength to stop his beast from going after them.

Oh, he knew what the man really was. King of his Murder to all his cronies, but he was nothing but a coward. A phony with a crown and Thor didn't give a fuck about his position. His beast was old school when it came to revenge, and he demanded blood for the bruises that asshole had put on Nica's sweet face.

Weeks wasted, snarled his Demon Wolf.

The animal was right. He'd spent weeks dancing around his feelings, staying away from the only woman he had ever wanted. A woman he'd thought was already mated. But here she was, standing in the otherwise empty garage and facing him down bravely. It seemed Nica wanted answers, too. But he kept his mouth shut until he knew he could speak without snarling at her. Only then did he speak.

"You said your mate hurt you. The day you fell."

"I did? Well, I mean, we were supposed to be mated, but he already had two mates when he brought me to the trailer park, and, um, I j-just couldn't."

"I'm going to need you to explain what you mean by that, Nica. Start from the beginning."

He watched her process his request, waited until

she nodded her head in agreement. Thank fuck. he didn't know what he would have done if she refused him. Her assent was step one in the quest to find out more.

Of course, it was made that much more difficult since the movement of her head had the long curls down her back and around her shoulders flutter about like magic. She was pretty before, but fuck, right then, she was beautiful. He didn't know when she'd pulled the elastic band from her hair, but he preferred it this way. All loose and wild and perfect.

He had to work hard not to reach out and run his fingers over it, not through it. Curly hair demanded a different approach. Despite shaving his head, Thor understood her curls worked differently than waves or straight hair, and he would never want to hurt her.

Not ever.

"I guess it started with my mother," she finally began after some seconds of careful consideration.

"Your mother?" he asked.

Thor was incredulous. How did her mother have anything to do with this? Patience, he reminded himself. Nica was not like the other women in his life, and he would do well to remember that.

"Ravens are different from most Shifters. We

tend to live solitary lives, unless paired up. And only then do we live with our immediate families. We don't gather in groups because there just aren't very many of us," she explained.

"Ravens and Crows don't usually live together?" he asked.

"Sometimes, but not always. There aren't that many Crows either. Not like Wolves and Bears. Anyway, when Dad died, it was just me and Mama for a while. She worked at a small diner waitressing, and after I finished high school, I worked there too after my community college classes. It was a tough couple of years. Quiet, boring, until the Crows came through."

"Came through how?"

"Motorcycles. Not like that, though," she said, nodding towards his hog and he thought he saw excitement light her gaze for a moment. "They aren't wealthy, and well, I hate to speak ill, but they don't take care of their things like you all do."

Thor's Wolf looked on approvingly, but he needed to reserve judgement for when she finished. So far, it had been nothing but the truth. Even if his supernatural senses couldn't hear a lie, there was something so innately honest about Nica. Even when she was hiding something.

And yes, there was something else she was trying to keep hidden. He wanted so badly to use his sight, to ferret it out of her. But there was another side of him that wanted her truths freely given.

Wait. Don't force it.

So he stood and listened to her talk. Her Maryland accent was subtly different from the Jersey girls he was used to hearing, but he liked it. Like her tone and the cadence of her speech. Nica was naturally soft-spoken.

Sweet girl. Pretty girl.

"Then he started coming to the diner more often, and one day it was like he was there every afternoon during my shift after my classes," she mumbled through that part.

"You went to college?" Thor asked.

"Yep. I know I don't sound very educated, but yes, I did. I liked school. A lot."

She shrugged as if it were something to be embarrassed about, and Thor frowned. She deserved a chance to follow her dreams. If that meant going back to school, then why the fuck not?

"First, I think you sound just fine, Nica. Real fine. Smart, funny, caring. I've been watching you for weeks, and I don't think you've ever said an unkind word about anyone," he murmured.

"That's not true. I called Leo a fathead one day when he criticized my shot pouring."

"Leo is a fathead. So again, you were just being honest," he told her with a grin he couldn't hide if he wanted to. "Second, how old are you?"

"Oh, I'm twenty-six. I know it's still young, but I feel older sometimes. Much older," she mumbled, and his heart squeezed for another reason.

Twenty-six. Fucking hell. It seemed the Fates were more fucked up than he'd thought. Dire Wolves aged even slower than other Shifters, and Thor was almost twice Nica's age, though he looked about thirty tops.

"Third, what did you study?" he asked, scrubbing a hand roughly over his face. He needed to focus on something other than their age difference.

"Well, I had to take some regular classes like English and Math. But I was really into these horti-culture classes," she told him.

He watched, interested, as Nica's cheeks turned pink, and she averted her gaze. Was she embar-rassed? He grinned and asked her for more details, delighted when she spoke about hydroponics and raised garden beds, experimenting with different soil types and experimental filtration systems. There were so many layers to this woman, he mused. And he wanted to know them all.

"Horticulture? Wow! I wouldn't have guessed that," Thor replied.

He had one hand on top of his head, rubbing the stubble that had grown that day, and the other on his hip as he stood shaking his head and grinning at her. It felt like a present, this little snippet of information she was giving him about herself. Yeah, like a really good present, and he liked it so much, he wanted more. But Nica was just staring, so he dropped his hand.

"What is it?" he asked.

"Nothing," she blurted, and he could scent her embarrassment now.

"Nica, what is it?" he repeated.

"You just have a really nice smile, is all. Like a really, really nice smile. And you don't do it very often. Smile, I mean. So I don't get to see it very often. It surprised me, but like, in a really nice way. You look good when you smile. Well, you look good all the time, but you look fantastic when you smile, and I am talking way too much now, so I am going to shut up," Nica finished with a popping sound on the final *p*. Now Thor was smiling even harder.

"Tell me why you said that Crow was your mate,"

he said, needing to know before he did what he was dying to do.

"H-he told me he was. That is, he started courting me. He was sweet at first. Said all the right things, brought me gifts, won my mother over right away. She couldn't have said yes to him when he suggested a pairing any quicker than she did. At least, that was what I thought."

"Did you love him?"

"I thought so," she replied honestly. "But understand, I'd never had a boyfriend till Jack. The things I should have questioned, I didn't because I thought maybe I was wrong. Maybe that was what love was supposed to be. He hid stuff. He left for days on end. He told me what he liked me to do, how I should act and what I should wear, and I tried to make him happy. But he would leave, and when he came back, he'd be different. Sometimes happy. Sometimes cruel. I was very green, you see. Jack liked to make fun of me for not knowing about stuff," she confessed.

That black rage inside Thor grew as she told her story, but he held it in. He did not want to make it any worse for Nica. Keeping his Demon Wolf hidden was necessary. So, he zipped his lip and listened. He wished he could smile for her right then, the way she'd liked, but that grin was nowhere to be found.

Not then, anyway.

"Mama conducted a promise ceremony that spring under a cherry tree in the local park. He gave me a ring, and I was floating on air, thinking I was gonna be married and mated. We went to a motel, and we, well, you know," She muttered, cheeks red now, and he could scent her discomfort. "Jack was so angry after. He made fun of me, said I didn't know a damn thing about being a mate. After that humiliating experience, he brought me to the Pine Murder trailer park, where I was placed with two other women. I didn't know till after he took off that they were his mates, and that I was going to be his third."

By the time Nica finished speaking, Thor was trembling with rage. That motherfucker. He'd taken something precious from her, and instead of being grateful and easing her into it, he'd humiliated and abused her trust. Thor's fury intensified. And her mother! How could a mother give away her innocent young daughter like that? It was revolting, and more black fury filled him. But there was something he didn't understand.

"He had other mates. Living mates and he wanted you, too?"

"Yes. Ella and Denise are both alive and both wear his mating mark. Crows don't bite like other predatory Shifters, they scratch and offer a token. He got Denise on the right side of her face, and Ella on her left. Used to call them a matched pair," she whispered, shivering before she continued.

"Poor Ella was not well when I got away. He broke them, and he wanted to break me." Horror leaked into her voice.

"Nica," Thor said her name and took a step closer to her.

"They're both just broken shells of the women they once were. I thought I was lucky when Denise got pregnant. He left me alone for years, but then she lost the baby, and then Ella got sick. He still has no sons, you see. So suddenly, he wanted me again, but I refused him. I swear to you, I refused him. I was so afraid Thor, so afraid would break me, too," she confessed, tears running down her cheeks.

"He didn't break you, Nica," Thor interrupted, taking her by the upper arms.

He couldn't stand to see her pain, but she needed to see the other side of it. He had to help her see. And he would if it took him all his life, he would. That was his vow to her, though he didn't voice it.

"You got free, Nica. You aren't broken."

"I ran. I was afraid, and I ran, and I just left them!"

She hiccupped, her blue eyes were wild, and her tear-stained cheeks were ruddy. Nica trembled beneath his fingers and something darkly possessive grew within him. His protective instinct went into overdrive, and he growled deep and low before reining back the Wolf. When his eyes met hers again, she was no longer crying, but shivers seemed to run through her and into him.

"Listen to me, Domenica Corvo, you are not broken. You did the best you could in a terrible situation. You got the fuck out, Nica. You got out! And I am so fucking proud of you," he told her, and pride filled his veins, lacing his voice.

Brave. Fierce. Badass female.

"You shouldn't cuss," she whispered, eyes glued to his mouth, and that warm feeling inside him grew some more.

Thor couldn't have stopped what was going to happen next even if he wanted to, and he had to be honest with himself, he did not want to stop it. Not at all. He closed the space between them, lifting one hand to cup Nica's cheek. Her big, blue eyes stared, unblinking, as he slowly lowered his head to hers. He needed to make sure she had ample time to step back, to tell him no if that was what she wanted.

Please don't tell me no.

Thor continued his advance, nuzzling her nose and tipping her head to the side before pressing his lips ever so softly to hers. That warm buzz he felt whenever he was around her was focused now, right on their meeting lips. Then he kissed her harder, pressing against her mouth, waiting till she parted her lips on a sigh, and he delved inside.

Mine.

CHAPTER 8

He's kissing me. Thor Ulger is kissing me.

He closed the space between them. Those hard, hot muscles she'd been coveting for weeks pressed into her soft body, as he ever so slowly pressed his lips against hers with soft, tender kisses. Her whole body teetered on the edge, but she didn't move. Didn't want to scare him away. Thor kissed her sweetly, as if he was waiting for her to push him away.

Yeah, right.

Like she was going to do that. Didn't he know how much she wanted this? To be the woman who got to kiss a man like him? Those first few kisses were everything to Nica. She sensed him holding back, though, and that was not okay. She wanted all of Thor, not some watered-down version. Nica needed more.

She didn't have to wait long, thank goodness. As if sensing her desire, Thor growled, crashing his mouth against hers, and Nica moaned, helplessly accepting him, and holding on for dear life. It was all she could do while the man himself plundered her mouth like his Viking ancestors did to villages in the not so distant past.

Yes. More.

His scent enveloped her, Wolf, wood, and some musky spice that made her want to climb him like an oak. The kiss turned rough, demanding as he backed her against the wall, and she wondered what he would say if she told him she wanted him to strip her clothes off and make love to her just like this.

Her emotions were all over the place, and something inside told her this man could wreck her. It was nuts. She'd been living in fear of one man breaking her for so long, but a few weeks with the Dire Wolves, with him, and she was ready to throw all caution to the wind.

Nica had felt anchorless, helpless for so long, but in this moment with Thor, she felt grounded, truly grounded for the first time in her life. Thor's chest reverberated with that ever-present growl as she clung, kissing him back for all she was worth. True, she was unpracticed, but he did not seem to mind at all. She clutched his shoulders, tangling her tongue with his while pressing herself more fully against his body.

He was so big, so hot and hard. And so very good at this, she thought while he kissed her till her toes curled. Again, as if he'd read her mind, he lifted his head, ripping his shirt off so she could feel all those wonderfully warm muscles pressing up against her. Her shirt came next, then both their shoes and pants.

"Fuck, we should stop. I should slow down. Get you to a bed or something, at least," he growled, but she pulled him back down to her.

"Let me have this," she whispered, almost begging. "Let me have you just like this, Thor. Please, I need, gods, I need," she moaned, rubbing herself all over him wantonly, but unable to help herself.

"Fuck, you are so sexy. What do you need, angel? Tell me," he commanded.

Nica gasped when she felt the cold wall against her back. Thor growled, lifting her like she weighed nothing at all. She moaned, wrapping her legs around his waist, loving the feel of his hardened length against her core. She was wet with need and embarrassed by it.

How long till he realized she was dripping for him? Would he shame her like Jack did that first and only time she had been with him? Of course not. Nica should know better. Trusting her gut, she decided to own the way he made her feel. This was something good, something rare, and beautiful. She wouldn't cloud it with thoughts of Jack. The foul man deserved zero seconds of her time.

"Your scent is driving me wild. But you gotta tell me what you want," Thor growled, and she moaned as he slipped her panties to the side and found her sopping wet secret. "Fuck, you're so wet for me, angel. So hot and tight. S'good."

Nica could hardly believe what was happening. Somehow, he'd gotten through all her hangups with his magic kisses and skilled hands. He was moving now, inside her panties, those thick fingers parting her slick folds, Thor was doing what no man had ever done. Thor was giving her pleasure.

He used his thumb to caress her swollen nub while he pushed one, then two fingers into her core. It had been so long since anyone touched her, and never, never ever had it felt so good.

She was wound so tight, her mouth opened as she clung to his neck. Thor seemed to love it, though, and he kept on stroking her with her panties pushed to the side. The fabric was hopelessly soaked now. He growled, sucking in her neck and back to her tongue, moving his hips in time with his efforts.

"Oh gods, Thor, that feels so, oh gods!" Nica cried out and moaned, unable to finish her thought as pleasure exploded, pulsing through her veins.

"One," he grunted.

He kissed her again, rewarding her, it seemed. Nica continued to ride his hand, embracing the sharp pleasure and the mini aftershocks he had so thoughtfully gifted to her. Through her lusty fog, she realized he was counting off her orgasms.

Holy cow.

Her experience with men was pretty nil, but she had to admit, it was a mighty turn on for a guy to exude such utter confidence in his ability to pleasure her. Nica's eyes widened, a disappointed groan sounding from her lips as her sex clenched on air, missing his invasion once he slid his fingers from her channel.

"Fucking delicious, angel," he growled.

Thor slipped his two fingers, still glistening with her pleasure, into his mouth and sucked them dry. Holy hell. She had no idea how hot that would be, and watching his eyes dilate with hunger sent pools of moisture flooding her crevice.

"You ready for two?" Thor asked, backing up a step but holding her still against the wall.

She looked down to see his engorged cock in his fist. Thor watched her watching him as he placed the broad head against her needy sex. She'd only ever done this once, and it was horrible, embarrassing, but even acknowledging that, she had to admit she never wanted Jack the way she wanted Thor.

"If you want me to stop, Nica, tell me now. Once I do this, there is no going back," he growled, black eyes burning into hers.

"I want this. I want you," she said automatically, owning her truth the only way she knew how.

"Mine," he growled.

Then he fed her his cock inch by delicious inch until he was seated all the way to the hilt. He pressed his whole body against her, cupping her face and holding her still. He was so big, but patient with her, giving her time to adjust to his size and girth.

"Damn angel, you feel better than I thought you would," he grunted, kissing her then as if she were something precious to him.

Had he been thinking about her like this? Holy cow. This big, beautiful man had been imagining sex with Nica, and suddenly she felt like a goddess instead of a silly girl with almost zero skills to offer the sexy as sin male. Sensations flooded her system, he was so big stretching her till it burned. But it was a good feeling, very good.

She wanted him to move so damn bad, but the beast of a man would not be rushed. Oh, she felt his animal inside him, knew the Demon Wolf was there, waiting just as she was. Then suddenly, he pulled out, pushing back in, taking her in long, deep, hard strokes. Nica had no idea people could do this standing up, let alone for as long as they did. But his strength was immense and his stamina double that. In the end, Thor made her come three more times. Each time was better than the last.

Hours later, he carried her outside with a clean towel draped over her naked body and didn't stop moving until he laid her down on the king sized bed inside his room in the Pack House. Once there, he crawled up her body, kissing, nibbling, tasting her flesh until she was panting and moaning beneath him.

"You taste so good, angel. Sweeter than the sweetest strawberry jam," he growled, kissing her *there*.

"Thor," she yelled, pulling on his head, his ears, whatever she could grab.

Nica yelled, moving up on her elbows, eyes

glued to him as he parted her folds with his tongue. Her heart was beating so hard it was liable to come right out of her chest with the things he was doing to her. Big hands pushed against her thighs, holding them open as he ravaged her pussy with his mouth.

How did he know how to do that? She couldn't even imagine another man impaling her on his tongue, making her see stars. Jealousy slapped at the recesses of her mind, but she pushed those hateful thoughts away. They had no place there with them. Just because she'd had an unfortunate past didn't mean he had.

She couldn't fault him for having women before her. He changed angles, filling her with his fingers while lapping at her clit. It was not long before she was moving again, grinding her sex on his face as she screamed his name, chasing her orgasm this time. It was too much.

He was licking her with steady swipes of his tongue until she thought she would fall apart into a million pieces. She couldn't do that, could she? Fear and curiosity filled her, and Nica pulled on his head. Thor stopped, looking up curiously at her.

"Did I hurt you?" he asked, his lips glistening with what she knew was her essence.

"No," she shook her head. "But no one ever, I mean, I never—"

A wicked grin split his face, and Thor kissed her pussy again, the same way he did her mouth. He lifted his mouth, eyes fixed on hers.

"You taste so good, angel. This is natural. It's good. I love the way you taste and I'm gonna make you feel so good, I swear it. Lemme have you. Lemme make you feel good," he growled, and she nodded, helpless to do otherwise.

Thank goodness for that. Trusting him was easier than it should have been, but Nica never felt anything as miraculous as Thor feasting on her pussy. His entire body seemed to reverberate with the steady growl he hadn't been able to dismiss, and the resulting vibrations had her flying over the edge sooner than she ever could have imagined.

In all her life, she never orgasmed multiple times in one night. Not even with the tiny clitoral stimulator she'd gotten in a swag bag from a birthday party she went to when she'd turned seventeen. Hiding that from her mother had been tricky, but she did. Otherwise, she might not ever have known what satisfaction felt like.

Of course, nothing compared to Thor. Her sex clenched around him when he finally reared up and gave her his dick. So long and thick, he hit all the right spots as he pressed inside. Nica moaned at how good he felt, filling and stretching her to capacity. It was like she was made for him. Her body was designed to fit his to a T.

"You were made for me," he growled in her ear as he rocked into her with deep, powerful strokes.

"You. Are. Mine. Nica, do you hear me? Mine. Now, tell me. Say it, angel," he grunted, and she nodded.

"Yes. Yours," she murmured, wishing with all her heart he meant those words for always and not just right now.

She felt like his. At least, she did right then. But Nica knew better than to hang her hopes on dreams of the future. This time, she would be smarter. This time, she would just live in the moment.

Enjoy the ride but hold on to your heart.

CHAPTER 9

Words of wisdom she'd heard somewhere, though she could not recall who'd said them. Nica wasn't the type of woman to hop from bed to bed. This was special. This was big. She would never forget the way Thor made her feel, even after he inevitably walked away. She would always remember this and him.

Regret was not something Nica was fond of. Though she regretted Jack and the Murder, she would never regret this or her time together with Thor. Living in the moment was something she strived for, and this right here was one helluva moment.

Tension started once more in her core, and Nica's whole body began to tighten around him.

Every move he made pushed her closer, closer, closer, until she was right there in the middle of a torrential downpour of pleasure.

"Thor!" she yelled, scratching his shoulders, followed by a loud, "ouch!"

Her Raven cawed inside her mind's eye just as a sharp pain stung her shoulder. But that feeling was soon overshadowed by another, second building of pleasure threatening to explode inside her until suddenly—*it did.*

White lights danced behind her eyes as she skyrocketed into oblivion, holding onto Thor for all she was worth. Thor reared up, his eyes completely obsidian, with no hint of white. It should have scared her, but Nica was too stunned by the sharp beauty of his face as he pounded into her.

The things he was doing, the feelings she was feeling, Nica just couldn't verbalize it. It was impossible for her to comprehend, but so damn poignant. Tears pricked her eyes as her pleasure intensified and Thor's rhythm turned jerky. He threw his head back and roared as the most intense orgasm she ever felt encapsuled them both. Thick jets of warm cum filled her, and Nica gasped at how right this felt.

Everything that happened before seemed to fall away. Her past. His. All of it. Nothing else mattered except for what was happening between them. Thor cupped her cheek with one hand, using the other to hold himself up so as not to crush her, but she wished he would. She welcomed his weight, loved the feel of his heavily muscled body pressing her down onto the mattress.

His black eyes glittered down at her, the look on his face as he worked to even his breathing was so serious, so full of awe, and she wondered if she looked the same. Everything was different now. She felt it in the air, a sort of charged energy that wrapped itself around her. Ravens didn't have a lot of lore about mates, but right then, she wished Thor was hers.

"Nica," he whispered reverently, dipping down to kiss her gently.

It was the smallest of touches, really, but it sent her heart pounding. He didn't seem done with her. Not yet anyway. A spark of hope ignited in her chest. Her experience with Jack had been hard and cruel, nothing like this. But it had left her so jaded.

She had to let that go. It was the past, and Thor was here in the now with her. He wasn't Jack. And she wasn't the same naïve girl she'd been. It was not wrong for her to want Thor. And she did want him.

Even more, she wanted him to want her back for longer than just this night.

"Want you," he whispered. "Want you so damn bad. Always."

His words were like music to her ears, and her body reacted to them predictably. Heating, warming, wetting just for him. She'd never felt so connected to another person, and she realized she was all in with him. The man could have her body, heart, and soul if he wanted her. What a frightening and wonderful thought that was, she mused.

Nica wanted him again, hoped he would take her fast and hard. That way, she could try to reconcile these new and scary emotions. The responding rumble in his chest and hardening of his cock still buried inside her told Nica he felt the same. But then someone knocked on the door, intruding on this sacred moment.

"Thor, that Crow came by with his lackeys. They're waiting across the highway behind the gas station, man. He says it's neutral ground. Says he wants his mate back, too," Cole told them. "Derrick wants you there," the Dire Wolf finished.

Thor and Nica remained quiet, but the moment was gone. She listened to the sounds of Cole's heavy footsteps walking away. That and the silence filled her ears, but he was gone before she even had time to protest Cole's use of the word *mate* in relation to her and Jack.

Nica was never the Crow King's mate. Not when he was courting her, not when he bedded her, and not when he beat her. Not ever.

Nothing could have told her that more than the way she'd responded to Thor's touch. The second the man known as the Demon Wolf of the Dire Wolf MC touched her, it was like a switch had gone off inside her. Nica's entire being seemed to recognize him.

His manner of speaking, the way he told her in no uncertain terms, he wanted her, was something she had never had from a man. Then there was her response. Her body welcomed his in a way she would have never thought possible. Thor was big and sexy, and rough around the edges, but with her he was direct, tender, and attentive.

Her skin heated, thinking about what they'd been doing together for hours now. She would have given anything to spend the entire night wrapped around him like a boa constrictor if only Cole hadn't knocked on the door. Just like that, the burning emotion she'd seen in Thor's eyes was extinguished.

He pulled out of her, leaving her cold and bereft

as he got out of bed. Whatever passion had burned so brightly between them moments ago had dulled now to a muted flame. Nica sat up, watching him with sad eyes.

"Where are you going?" she asked.

"To deal with this," he growled.

"It's not your problem, Thor. I'll go—"

"Not my problem? Nica, you're mine."

"I can try to reason with him," she said, avoiding his statement and hating the hope that rose within her. *Yes*, she wanted to say, *I am yours, but for how long?*

"No," Thor grunted, shaking his head. "I don't want you near that fucker. You stay here."

He pulled on jeans and a shirt, and she watched the play of muscles helpless to do otherwise. Her body was sore in places she didn't even know she had, but Nica would not have traded the last few hours with him for anything else in the world. Everything was all a jumble. Still, she refused to sit still and stay like an obedient puppy. Nica was a Raven, not a dog.

"Look, this is my mess. If you go, I go."

"Fucking hell, Nica," he growled, and turned to her so quickly he stopped her in her tracks.

Thor's eyes bled to black, and she felt a sudden

weight pressing down on her. Nica's shoulder burned fiercely while he glared at her, his powerful body flexing as he tried to keep his control in place. She looked down at her aching shoulder, finally taking stock of herself. Nica gasped at what she saw.

"You bit me," she whispered, shocked that she hadn't realized it.

"I told you. You are mine. You agreed, Nica." he growled, and her heart squeezed tight.

"Biting is the same as claiming to Wolves, right?" she asked, still trying to wrap her head around it.

"Fuck, I thought you understood," he cursed, rubbing the top of his head.

"Explain it to me," she demanded, wondering where she found the gumption to question him like that.

"Explain it to you?" he asked, his eyes blazing, that growl echoing in the room. "You. Are. Mine. Explanation over."

Nica knew she shouldn't like it when he said that. Something about feminism and being independent. It was all the females of the Dire Wolf Pack talked about. And a sassier group of females Nica had never met. Still, something primal and deep inside her recognized his claim, and reveled in it.

Lucy was the best. The tiny Alpha fem was

always giving her mate hell one minute, then making goo-goo eyes at him the next. Sheila was the same with Leo. Though Ariella and Brock were slightly more complicated and openly worshipped each other, while Tracey and Phoenix were all about traveling the globe and visiting when they could. Gwen was still managing her new Wolf, and Weylin was a surprisingly kind mentor, but their love was off the charts.

Nica had spent the last few weeks getting to know this close-knit Pack, and she'd been pleasantly surprised to find the females all had a say in what went down. That was the total opposite of how the Murder was run.

But back to his possessive declaration, honestly, Nica had heard the others say similar things to each other, but she never understood it. Now, with Thor standing in front of her naked and proud, his thick erection jutting out from between his legs, staking his claim with words as he had with his body, Nica just about melted into a puddle of goo at his enormous feet.

And why shouldn't she? Sassy or not, none of the females there seemed to mind it one bit when their larger-than-life mates came in, dropping proclamations of outright ownership and hauling them off to ravage them well into the night. Nope. In fact, those lucky women seemed to live for those moments.

You can too, her Raven whispered. *Mine.*

"But what does being yours mean to you, Thor?"

"There's no time now—"

"The heck you say! Look, Mr. Tall Dark and Tattooed, you said I'm yours. Tell me what that means!" she demanded, chest heaving with her sudden anger.

Thor paced a moment, then turned to her, those Demon Wolf eyes of his glittering dangerously. He was so damn handsome. So big and powerful. Thor just took up all the space in the room, leaving her with one helluva view, she had to admit.

"Okay, you want to know what it means? Fine," he grunted, freezing her in place with his laser like stare. "It means you let me have you, angel. Now, you're mine. And I have no intention of letting you go."

"Okay then," she mumbled, swallowing hard. "I'm yours.," Nica agreed aloud, her voice stronger. "Now, let me go to the meeting with you."

"No!" he snapped. "Fuck, Nica, I am sorry. I don't mean to yell. But it is dangerous."

"I don't understand, Thor. I want to be with you to clear this up. Why can't I come with you?"

She started towards him, but Thor stopped her with one hand and ran the other over his face. The air felt heavy again, and she swore she saw the air around him shimmer and pulse. He blinked a few times, his eyes returning to normal before he looked at her again.

"Thor?"

"Nica, please understand the Demon Wolf is feeling fiercely protective of you right now."

"Your Wolf wants to protect me," she replied, and she almost dropped the sheet she had wrapped around her body.

"If you go out there looking like you do, hair tousled, lips swollen, smelling of sex and me, I'll tear the throat out of every one of those motherfuckers before Derrick could even think to stop me. Understand?"

Truth.

Shifters had an ear for lies, and every word out of his mouth rang with the truth. Nica swallowed hard. Thor was trying to protect her from his Wolf, from the one everyone called Demon. But Nica wasn't afraid of him. His animal was possessive of her, and something deep inside her approved. She nodded her head, wanting to offer him comfort. But Nica didn't say anything. She didn't have a chance.

Thor was already crossing the room, looking powerful and determined. He slammed his lips into hers, taking her mouth in a fierce, savage kiss that hurt her lips, but in the best way possible. Those big, strong hands she loved gripped the back of her neck as he kissed her, stamping himself on her one more time before he had to go.

"Wait for me here. Say it," he commanded.

"I'll wait."

"That's my angel. I'll be back soon," he murmured, turning around before he could see her swoon.

Why was that such a serious turn on? She had no idea. All Nica knew was she was squirming by the time he adjusted himself in his tight jeans and turned. The man sure knew how to fill out that well-worn denim. His jeans were so tight, they were molded to his long legs and fit perfectly. The tight, long-sleeved shirt he wore was black, as usual, and clung to his musculature like a second skin.

Nica's mouth watered. He looked like a Viking warrior, all tattooed and scarred. They called him Demon, and she knew why. But to her he wasn't a Demon, he was an avenging angel. Her avenging angel. But Thor didn't look at her as he slipped his feet inside his boots. She waited for him to say something, but his hard lips remained closed.

Her heart squeezed, and she felt unsure and anxious. He'd claimed her with his bite, but she still did not understand the full meaning. Crows and Ravens didn't mate for life, but Nica would be crushed if he let her go. How was she going to survive this? How would she ever survive him leaving her?

Darn it. She was thinking too much. Over complicating things with her runaway thoughts and lack of confidence. The man called her his, that must mean something, right? Should she leave while he was gone? Go back to her room?

She had no experience with this kind of thing. Had no idea how to act. She wanted to make him happy but had no idea what he was expecting from her. Right when she was about to fly off into a full-blown panic, and before he walked out the door, he turned to face her. Thor's dark eyes found hers, and Nica stilled. Her Raven settled down, even as emotions flooded her system. Nica wasn't going anywhere.

Thor asked her if she understood what he meant with his oddly specific account of what he would do should she walk across the street to the meeting place. In his eyes, she saw his Demon Wolf, saw the possessive beast staring at her with hunger in his impossibly dark eyes., and something else. Something dark and deadly.

Somehow, letting Thor between her legs and wearing his bite mark had turned the Pack's Enforcer into a giant murdery powder keg. What else was there to understand?

Okay. Nica swallowed, certain now she understood what he meant.

Kinda. Mostly. Gulp.

CHAPTER 10

The Demon Wolf snarled and snapped inside of him. The giant brindled beast wanted out. He wanted to savage the motherfucker who'd put hands on Nica. The animal was dying to punish the assholes who participated in that cruel and savage beating she'd received, along with the cowards who stood by and let it happen.

Grrrr.

Of course, he couldn't do that. Derrick would not allow it. His Alpha was already there. The true image of leadership, standing tall and strong, his power obvious to everyone there. But Thor was not concerned with Derrick or that piece of shit Crow at the moment.

He was busy battling the *other* as he traipsed

across the semi-busy highway to the lot behind the gas station. Dark images of shadow spirits floated around him as he walked to meet with the Pine Murder and their cowardly leader. Their desperate pleas and gravelly whispered bargains pounded against his head.

Whispers full of evil suggestions slithered in his ear, and he fought with his Wolf for control. Unlike his human side, the Demon Wolf had no qualms about gutting the men who'd hurt what was his. But Thor did not live in his fur alone. He could not give in to those spirits whose cries and moans he decidedly ignored whenever he crossed the veil.

They were the cursed ones. The ones who wanted vengeance and threatened to pull him down into the darkness forever. It was a battle sometimes, to return to this side of the veil where the living ruled, and the spirits whispered to those few who had the sight. But not anymore. Thor belonged here in the light with Nica. He just had to make sure these assholes understood she was his now.

Not theirs. She would never be theirs.

Thor canted his head, watching the two groups of males face off behind the gas station, just across the road from the Pack House and their bar. Neutral ground. That was what they thought they had by going there, but Thor had a surprise for them. He didn't give a fuck whose land they stood on. If they came for Nica, he would gut them all.

He walked over to them unhurriedly, listening with all his senses. No one had spoken a word yet. They just stood, waiting he imagined for him to arrive. Derrick stood half a foot taller than the Crow King.

Good Alpha. Strong.

His animal approved of Derrick, always had. He was easily the tallest man there, save for Thor. He knew the male had his back and normally, neither he nor his Demon Wolf would ever think of questioning him.

Until now.

Why the fuck did the Alpha agree to meet with these needle dicks? They hurt his Nica. Demanded she return to them when Thor would never let that happen. Fuck. He was losing it. Thor was acting like a possessive fucking caveman, but he never claimed to be anything else. No, he wouldn't ever send her back, but more than that, he knew she didn't want to go back.

"Great. The giant is here. Now, can we talk about you giving me my mate back?" the King whined like a petulant child.

Grrrr.

"I was not aware we had your mate, Jack Bran-wen, King of the Pine Murder. Perhaps you have a photo? A description? Anything handy, so we might help you search for this lost mate."

Derrick addressed the man whose neck Thor was itching to break with as much respect as propriety demanded. But he did not bother to disguise his loathing for the woman beating piece of shit. And that was why Thor loved the man.

"You listen to me, Wolf. She's here, I saw her—" Jack said, spittle flying from his lips.

A fierce growl interrupted the byplay, and Thor stepped forward, forcing the man to back up. He was rude and disrespectful to their Alpha, and the beast in him would not tolerate such blatant discourtesy. His Pack mates loosed similar growls, though none held his venom. Thor kept advancing, forcing the King to retreat like the coward he was. No, he was not above using his size to intimidate, especially in these circumstances.

"You will address our Alpha with the respect he is due," growled Thor, holding on to his anger by a thread.

"You can't do this. I came here under a banner of peace, but I will bring this to the Council if I must—"

"Peace? You beat a woman for refusing your bed. You came here with your men, walked into our bar to force her to go with you, and you call that peace?"

"Thor," Derrick said his name. "Leave off," he commanded.

Thor was breathing heavily, wrestling with his Demon Wolf, but the beast owed fealty to their Alpha. He stopped short, holding onto the fist he so desperately wanted to bury in that asshole's face. Derrick had saved the man from a broken nose, but there was nothing he could do about the permanent growl in Thor's throat.

"She is m—"

"No. She is not your mate," Thor stated, daring the Crow King to argue.

He did. But not with Thor. The pitiful excuse for a man couldn't seem to meet his eyes. Thor's growl got louder, and the Crow King stuttered. He imagined his eyes were full black now, glittering, and dangerous looking. Having the sight meant sometimes Thor could see a person's true nature. When he looked at the Crow King all he saw was darkness.

Grrrr.

The Crow blanched, the color leaving his face faster than rats fleeing a sinking ship. He looked back at Derrick, as if Thor's Alpha would take his side for some reason. Stupid, entitled coward that he was, he probably did think that. Thor just shook his head.

Of course, he can't look at us. He knows we want to rip his black heart out of his chest, his Demon Wolf grinned inside his mind's eye.

"*Alpha,*" Jack sneered the title. "Domenica Corvo is my mate. She is a liar if she says otherwise! I signed a marriage contract with her mother for her hand, and it is binding. By Crow law, Domenica Corvo is my claim," Jack said, handing one of his men an envelope.

One of his Crows, a lanky, thin male, held the envelope out to Derrick with shaking hands. Fucking guy had to be twenty years old, if that. Cole stepped forward and took the thing, handing the envelope to Derrick. Thor made no effort to move. His black eyes stayed pinned on the Crow King while the slimy, unworthy male continued to argue his so-called rights.

"I will look this over, but Mr. Branwen? You should know I don't give two fucks about Crow law. The Dire Wolf MC lives outside of Shifter Council law, as we have for hundreds of years."

"Yeah, well, you broke off from your MC, *Wolf,*"

the Crow King replied with a smirk. "You can't claim their privilege anymore."

"You know, it's interesting you think those ties are so easily broken, Crow. You think because we settled here, we are no longer part of the greater Dire Wolf MC, but you could not be more wrong. If I were you, I would think about that before deciding what route you wish to take with us," Derrick commented, inclining his head to the Pack.

"I will have her back!" the Crow King shouted, and Thor paused, only moving forward when Derrick slapped a hand on his shoulder.

The rest of the Dire Wolves walked behind the two of them, giving the Murder their backs in the ultimate *fuck you* someone could give to another Shifter. Thor wanted to be the last to leave, but it turned out to be no simple thing to walk away. His entire body trembled with pent up anger.

His *other* pulsed and growled. That part of him watched hungrily, waiting for him to act. The shadow spirits grew louder, egging him on to do something foolish. His Demon Wolf allowed him to commune with the spirits and granted him use of his *sight*, but it was not always good.

Right then, Thor's other was a hungry thing. It craved vengeance, demanded he pay back the Crow

King for every scratch, bruise, and for the dislocated arm he had given Nica. But his good Alpha had given an order, he'd bolstered him up, and led Thor away. Yes, he would find peace and solace in obeying that command. Didn't want to return to Nica with blood on his hands. Not when their mating was so new.

"The Council will hear about this, Wolf. If she is not returned to me by tomorrow, I will be back and I will bring war with me. She is mine, do you hear me? My mate," yelled the soon to be dead motherfucker.

He did not know how or when, and yes, Thor would obey his Alpha always, but that Crow was pushing him too far. Thunder roared in his ears. It was too loud for Derrick's newest Alpha command to take root.

"Thor—"

Too late. He blurred across the street the same second the Crow had stopped speaking, lightning fast, Thor moved, facing off with the piece of shit. He snarled, snapping his teeth as he grabbed the Crow King by the throat, dangling the male a good three feet off the ground.

"Let's get one thing straight, Crow. Nica is mine."

Mine, grumbled his Demon Wolf.

Derrick and the rest of the Pack jogged back to his side and the Alpha's hand clamped down on Thor's shoulder once more. He felt the man's innate power pulsing through their Pack bonds at his touch. Lucky for the Crow King, he still recognized his Alpha as his leader before he went and tore his head right off. A regret he felt immediately as he loosened his hold.

"Come on, man. We gotta go."

Thor completely released the male's throat and watched with more than a little satisfaction as the fucker hit the ground. He muttered a curse in the ancient language and spat on the floor next to where the Crow King gasped and struggled to catch his breath.

Once he was back on Pack land, the tension in his shoulders lessened a tad. He felt everyone's questioning eyes and concerning glances, but he shook them off. There was only one thing that could help him release his stress now. He needed to change shape, to run in his fur.

Without a sound, he let the Wolf take him. The clothes shredded right off his body as his enormous beast burst from his skin. Thor meant to run through the woods, but the soft gasp he heard from the side door had his big, lupine head turning around. Fuck, she saw his uncontrolled change. Worry over whether she would fear him now spiked his heart, but her eyes held nothing of horror as she watched him. Only wonder.

Nica. Mine.

Brave and beautiful, she stood watching him. His mate. A deep, satisfied rumble made its way past his lips as he trotted over to her. She had her hands over her mouth, her big blue eyes eating him up. Her happiness intensified the freshly fallen rain scent that seemed as much a part of her as the fresh bread and sweet summer jam he often associated with her.

"Oh Thor! You are so beautiful. I've never seen anything like you. A brindle Dire Wolf, well, I'll be," she murmured softly.

His animal preened under her warm praise. The beast liked her eyes on him, hungry and proprietorial. He liked them so much he wanted more. No, Thor demanded more. He needed her hands on him, so he bumped her gently with his head, allowing her sweet laughter to wash over him as he nudged her towards the door, away from prying eyes.

He never thought of himself as a jealous man, but there was something wildly possessive in how he felt about Nica. She closed the door to his bedroom behind them and kneeled on the rug by the recliner he had against the wall. He didn't know where she found the shirt she'd put on, but he liked her in his clothes.

"Can I touch your fur?" she asked, her eyes glowing with her animal.

To answer her question, Thor got down on his belly and crawled over to her. He knew he was big, and the last thing he wanted was to scare the woman. She squealed happily, reaching out with tentative hands, and running them over his back and neck.

Then he dropped his head in her lap and licked her elbow, making her giggle until she was giving him a good, long petting. She was wearing his shirt, so he didn't mind dirtying it, and even better, the little minx had nothing underneath it. He discovered that sweet little tidbit after he pushed his head down farther to investigate.

"Hey! Bad Wolf," she said, swatting his nose.

Thor's Wolf sneezed. He felt the air surrounding him shimmer as he swapped his Wolf's brindle fur for his human form. She was so fucking beautiful it hurt to look at her, but he couldn't turn away. He wouldn't. Not for anything. Nica was part of him now. Somehow, the curvy goddess had gotten beneath his skin. She was big now, important in a way he never knew possible.

"You swatted my nose, angel. Time for payback," he growled playfully.

"No fair! You were sniffing my hoo ha!" Nica yelled, but she was also laughing, and her eyes were sparkling with humor and something more.

"Gonna do more than sniff it, angel. I'm gonna lick that delicious little pussy until you're coming all over my face, begging for my dick. Then I'm gonna fuck you real good, just like you like, until you're screaming my name," Thor promised, his voice thick like gravel as he ran his hands up her luscious curves, divesting her of his shirt.

Her eyes grew hooded, the scent of her arousal perfumed the air. Thor could not wait a second longer. He tackled his sweet little mate to the ground like the predator he was, but he made sure she didn't get bumped or bruised. He wasn't a total asshole, after all.

"Thor,": she moaned his name, and he was a goner.

He kissed her until she clung to him in submission, opening her thick thighs and cradling him with her soft body. After a while, after Thor was finished driving them both crazy with only kisses, he slid down her body, ready to feast on her sweet strawberry jam flavored essence.

He knew the old cliché about cats liking cream. But the thing was, Thor was all Wolf. He was the total fucking opposite of a cat. But he also knew one thing for sure, he fucking loved eating her pussy. Loved lapping at her cream. And he would never stop licking at her until he'd downed every last drop, with his woman screaming his name and coming on his face.

Mine.

But it wasn't enough to lap at her. He needed to feel her come. So Thor fucked her with his tongue, using his nose to grind against her clit. Naughty girl that she was, Nica arched and tried to move against him, but he held her down with one hand on her hip, while keeping the other busy squeezing her sumptuous ass. Her pleasure was his only goal, but he was the one in charge. And from the way she panted and moaned, he knew he got that right.

Fuck, this woman was everything to him. For someone who knew virtually nothing about sex, she was more passionate and responsive than any of his previous experiences. Even thinking of sharing his body with another made him cringe and his Wolf snarl, but there wasn't anything he could do about it. Those women were in the past. Nica was his present, his future. She was everything.

"Thor, Thor, THOR!" she moaned his name, pulling on his head.

Her orgasm crested, making him feel like a god as she quivered and clenched around his tongue. Nothing was better to Thor than seeing the expression on Nica's face when she came and knowing he was the reason for it. He wanted to see it at least half a dozen times before the sun came up.

"One," he growled, and her blue eyes widened as he slid up her heated body.

"It's already five. You must be tired," she whispered, confused, but still accepting his mouth when he reached for a kiss.

"Not telling the time, angel. Counting your orgasms. So, how many you want before we go to sleep, angel?" he asked, ignoring her observation.

Thor didn't wait for her to answer. He was already pushing into her, feeling her walls clench and ripple as she started to come again, almost immediately. Fuck, he loved this woman. It was too soon, but so what? He was a Wolf with the *sight,* and for the first time in his life, he saw a future for himself. A future that revolved around a woman with curly dark hair, eyes like an October sky, and a heart of gold.

"Mine. Mine. Mine," he growled in time with his thrusts.

And when she came a third time on his cock, he followed suit. But still, it wasn't enough. Thor's cock grew hard again in seconds after he'd finished spewing cum into her womb. This time, instead of rutting her on the floor like a beast, he carried her to the bed. He needed to go slow. Needed her to feel what he felt.

"Damn, Nica. You really changed everything, didn't you?"

"What do you mean?"

"You're a miracle, you know that. You make me hope," he murmured, kissing her cheeks, her mouth, her neck.

"How, what do you hope?" she asked.

"You just give me hope, angel. Like there's a future for me now, here with you," he confessed, kissing her hard and deep.

Fuck, he was talking too much. He thrust his tongue into her hot cavern, mimicking what his cock was doing to her tight little pussy.

In and out. Slip and slide. Flex and withdraw.

And all he could think every time he had her was

more. More. More. MORE. He wanted all of her. Even as he stamped himself all over her, he still wanted everything. The thought of that Crow bastard coming there and demanding Nica as his claim made Thor's blood boil.

Fuck him.

Thor would not let that happen. Not ever. He needed a plan. A good one. Because if the Council came sniffing around for his mate, there would be trouble and it would be big. The only thing certain was Thor would never give Nica up. Not without a fight.

Mine.

CHAPTER 11

Nica woke to the sounds of hushed voices and a bright light. What the heck? Oh, someone had opened the window curtain. But who? Wait, her bedroom window was on the other side of the room, wasn't it? She yawned, taking a moment to reconcile where she was.

Dire Wolf Pack? Check.

The bedroom they gave me? Nope.

Thor's room? Yep.

Smiling with memories of how she'd spent the night filled her as she rolled over, dragging the sheet with her as she stretched. Sitting up, Nica blinked herself awake, then screeched like a crazy person. Not one, but four, four pairs of eyes were looking at her with matching expressions.

"Look who finally decided to join us!" Sheila barked, clapping her hands.

"Come on, darlin'. Upsy daisy. Your man has everyone up in arms this morning, and I am grumpy as fudge."

"Huh?" Nica asked, confused as all get by several things.

The least of which was not figuring out why the Alpha fem should be grumpy. She was gorgeous, had a mate, and three cubs, and a totes perfect life from Nica's point of view. The other females sighed in commiseration, But Nica just blinked.

"Well, what do you expect since this little mama still isn't allowed to have coffee?" Lucy grumbled.

"Oh," Nica muttered.

That made sense. Still, Nica grinned as she looked at one of the reasons the horrible *no caffeine rule* was in place. The pretty little cub was currently suckling from Lucy's left boob, while Ariella and Gwen bounced the other two reasons, *er*, cubs, in their arms to calm them while they waited for their turn to eat.

It was a sight, but it still did not explain why any of the women were in hers, *um*, Thor's bedroom. Nica cleared her throat and clutched the sheet up higher to hide her naked breasts from the crowd.

"We've already seen those tatas. Good for you, by the way! Oh, just a word of advice, get your man to shave or at least moisturize before he chaps them raw with that scruff of his," Ariella informed her with a sage nod.

Tracey and Gwen murmured in agreement, and Nica just stared. Were all the men in this Pack as randy as her own sexy as sin mate? Lucky women if they were. Ariella seemed to be waiting for a response, and the Lioness truly was exquisite with her mane of wild curly hair, not unlike Nica's, but that was where the similarities ended.

"Oh, I don't think I could say things like that to Thor. Besides, I like the way his scruff feels when he, *er*," she trailed off.

"Nuzzles you in your most sensitive places?" Ariella suggested.

"What?"

"She means when he's going down on that *poonanie*," Lucy supplied.

That did it. Every female in the room started snickering and giggling at the Alpha fem's use of that word. Even the babies gurgled. Nica wiped her eyes and tried to calm down before asking them what she really wanted to know.

"Well, that was fun. But ladies, why are you here?"

"Oh, well, the boys are going over that bit of paper that big nosed Crow brought with him, and it looks like the Council has reason to side with that horrible man seeing as how you and your mother signed it—"

"But I didn't know he had two other mates waiting back home. And I didn't love him. He didn't even like me! Jack Branwen is a dirty liar," she replied vehemently.

"Mm hmm, that is what Thor said, but Derrick isn't sure that matters. He is consulting with a Shifter lawyer on loan from the Macconwood Pack. Meanwhile, there is a little something we would like to do while the boys handle this business."

"Shouldn't we stay and help?"

"Nah. They're only just getting through the posturing portion of their meeting. Then will come the brainstorming, and I sure as hell don't wanna be here for the mansplaining," Ariella told her, and Nica had to admit she had a point.

"Okay, then, what do you want to do?"

"Well. After Lucy here is done feeding the triplets, we thought we'd go into town and have a real ladies' day out!" Ariella squealed.

"A what?"

"You know, we'll go into town and have a girls' only day. There is this new place called Heavenly Bodies and they have a full treatment spa. I already called and booked us the bridal party treatment package—"

"Bridal party? But I am not getting married," Nica replied, stunned.

"Oh, honey, it doesn't matter. You just got mated."

"No, I mean, I guess so, but we haven't had a chance to talk," she tried to explain.

But Nica could not get a word in. Those women ran roughshod right over her in the best possible sense, of course.

"Of course you didn't talk. Words still have no place in mine and Weylin's bedroom," Gwen mused, her eyes taking on a dreamy look as she spoke of her mate.

"Look, Nica, Thor gave you his bite mark, don't you know that means you are as good as married?" Sheila interrupted.

"It's true. Besides, mated is better," Tracey told her with a soft smile.

"I guess, I mean, Crows seem to throw that word around a lot, and even though I am a Raven, I hardly remember what my parents were like together when dad was alive. With Jack, it seemed like Mama picked him before I even had a chance to make up my mind. Everything happened fast, and I was confused, but I am not confused now. I want Thor. He's the only man I ever really wanted."

"Well, it's settled then. Congratulations," Lucy said, grinning as she swapped babies and boobs. "You should know, Dire Wolves are different from other Shifters. They are more powerful, they follow ancient rules, and when I tell you they mate for life, I mean it, honey. Thor is never gonna let you go. Anyway, come on. It'll be fun," she coaxed.

That was a lot to swallow, and though Nica had misgivings about what they'd all said about mating for life since those words had not exactly come from Thor, she couldn't help but agree a day out sounded just peachy.

"It will be super fun. Besides, tonight is bikini night at the bar. We need to get our wax on!" Sheila exclaimed.

"Okay," Nica said, finally giving in.

Her head was spinning by the time they stopped yammering. She got in the shower. Well, she was dragged and pushed into the bathroom by Gwen, then had a pair of leggings and a sweatshirt shoved unceremoniously at her when she was done. One by one, they filed out of the bedroom with Sheila practically frog marching her through the hall and into the living room.

"Nica? Are you okay?" Thor asked.

"Um, I think so—" was all she managed to say with Sheila pushing her forward in with a relentless grip on her arms.

"She's fine. We're going out for the day," Lucy replied, handing Derrick one of their babies, while the other women placed the other two in nearby bassinets.

"I pumped this morning, bottles are in the fridge. We should be back by three," Lucy told him before following them outside.

"Wait. What is going on?" Thor asked.

"Ladies' day out," Tracey repeated slowly.

Nica had to hide her grin. Thor looked like he wanted to say something, maybe ask her to stay home. But Nica had no idea what to do. She really could not refuse, what with the entire Pack going to bat for her and all. Besides, Sheila had an iron grip on her.

Nica barely had time to take in the intimidating males sitting in the living room, discussing her life without her. Of course, she knew Thor and Derrick, but the pair of identical twins were strangers. They smelled like Wolf, but different from the Dire Wolf MC.

One had on a charcoal gray suit, and seemed to never smile, while the other wore a t-shirt with a bone on it, and the words *I got a boner to pick with you* strewn across the top. He was grinning at them like a loon. Nica raised her eyebrows and shrugged, but if she thought Thor was going to rescue her this time, she was mistaken.

"Be careful, angel. Come home safe," he rumbled, his black eyes boring into hers.

Twenty minutes later, Nica forgot most of her questions as a large woman with a German accent named Helga started wrapping her body in a seaweed mask treatment. The smell was not altogether unpleasant, and she kind of liked the part where the matronly female had massaged her scalp before applying a conditioning treatment there.

Heavenly Bodies was run by a coven of Eastern European Witches, so they did not have to worry about letting things slip in front of the staff. Helga had assured them their room was private and soundproof, not to mention surrounded by magical protection wards.

The spa was also located smack dab in the middle of town, with tons of normals around, so Nica didn't have to worry about the Murder trying anything with so many onlookers.

Still, she'd felt like someone was watching her while they drove and then walked through the parking lot. But even if they were following her, keeping tabs, Jack was not that stupid. He knew better than to grab her out in public.

"Ohmygawd! I feel like a princess," Lucy squealed when Helga moved on to her.

"Princess of the mud people," Ariella snorted, only to get thwacked by Sheila on the butt.

"Shush it, Miss Kitty. This is the most relaxation I've had in weeks," the she-Wolf told her.

"With the way you and Leo go at it, go figure, Sheila. I mean, I'm surprised you can even walk with all the sexy times you two got going on," snarked Gwen.

"Catty!"

"Ha! As if Gwen isn't getting sexed up every night," Ariella pointed out.

"Damn straight, I am," the new Dire Wolf confirmed.

"OMG! Just look at you, Gwendolyn. A second ago, you were this cute little pious virgin coming into the roadhouse for a job. Now look at you! Weylin sure corrupted you. But now, come on, we're scaring Nica here and today was supposed to be about her," Lucy teased.

"Who me? Nah, I'm enjoying the banter, believe me. I didn't know women could be so sassy and frank and still be friends," she told them honestly.

"Well, damn," Lucy said, sitting up. "Look, Nica, I don't know how you were raised, but in this Pack we females have one solemn rule and that is to always have each other's backs, no matter how outrageously sarcastic and sassy we get!"

"That's right!"

"Preach, Lucy!"

Nica laughed and wiped her eyes as the others all clapped and hooted. These women were like nothing she'd ever seen, and she was so grateful they included her, it was like a dream come true. She joked and laughed, and sipped champagne with them while they got pampered by Helga and her team.

She did her best to enjoy her first ladies' day out, and it was wonderful. Truly, it was. Her mind kept wandering back to Thor and the confrontation with Jack. The last thing she wanted was for the Crow king to bring war to the Pack's doorstep.

These were good people. They'd welcomed her with open arms, gave her a job, and made her feel part of the Pack, even though she was a Raven and not a Wolf. When they returned to the Pack House late that afternoon, Nica got ready for work.

She'd bought a new pair of tight blue jeans and a pale purple crocheted bikini to wear for tonight's theme at Serious Moonlight. It was October, but working behind the bar meant constant movement, besides Shifters hardly ever felt the cold.

Thor was nowhere to be found, but Nica assumed she'd see him at work. It was difficult not to feel a tad bit abandoned, but then again, they'd burned pretty hot and heavy for their first time together. Maybe he needed a break.

She worried her lower lip, wondering if the big beautiful Dire Wolf had grown tired of her already. Jack's cruel words came back to haunt her after the first time she'd ever had sex. He'd said bedding her was rough and called her a puritan. She hadn't satisfied Jack, and he'd been rude and hurtful.

Yes, it wounded her pride, but now she was really worried. Thor had not texted or called her all day. He was nowhere to be found when she got back. Not knowing what to do, she'd gone to her bedroom, *not his*, to bathe and dress. The whole time, her gut felt tight and heavy, clenched with nerves.

What if she was bad at sex? What if she'd turned Thor off with her wanton enthusiasm and lack of experience?

So many what ifs, her Raven observed with a sharp caw.

The animal was tired and weary of being kept locked away, but Nica did not dare free her bird. Not yet. Not until the Murder stopped hunting her. Then another of Jack's favorite taunts flooded her brain.

"No one gets away from me, Domenica. You should know that before you run. I would rather see you dead than let you leave."

She stepped outside, about to walk across the lot to the bar, when she saw it. A single black feather sitting on the porch. Tied to it was a black rose. Nica gasped, picking up the hateful thing. She ran to the dumpster and threw it away.

"Nica? What's wrong?"

A scream tore from her throat before she could stop it. Hand over her heart, she recognized Thor as he came thundering towards her, running his hands over her body, arms, and legs, checking for damage.

"Nica? Talk to me, angel. Are you hurt?" he asked,

before tugging her to his warm, hard body and wrapping her up tight in his embrace.

"Thor," she murmured.

Was she hurt? No. She wasn't hurt. She was fine now.

Perfectly fine, she thought as she hugged him back.

CHAPTER 12

"Nica? What's wrong?"

Thor's heart almost hammered right outside of his body when he saw Nica run across the lot behind the bar. He raced after her, calling her name, only to startle her into screaming.

Fuck. He should have been more careful, but his Wolf was riding him hard. He needed to make sure she was all right.

"Nica? Talk to me, angel. Are you hurt?"

"Thor," she said his name, clinging to him once she recognized him.

Thank fuck. He'd never felt this level of concern for another person, and it was downright scary. Hugging her close after he assessed her condition, Thor exhaled the breath he'd been holding.

"What happened, angel? Talk to me."

He kissed her temple before drawing back to look at her face. She was pale and shaken, and his beast reared up, ready to attack whatever had threatened his sweet mate.

"There was a feather tied to a rose on the porch. It was Jack, I know it was Jack. He used to leave that sort of thing for me back when he was courting me. Only this time, the rose was black. It was black," she murmured, and her voice was thick with tears.

"Sonofabitch came on Pack lands," he growled, incensed beyond measure.

"It's worse than that, Thor. A black rose is bad," she whispered, shaking her head.

"What does that mean? It was black, so what?"

"Crows only leave black roses for the dead, Thor. This was a warning. He wants me dead."

Motherfucker.

"Shhh. You're okay. I got you, angel. You're safe," Thor reassured her, kissing her head and holding her close.

Nica was scared, that much was obvious. But there was something else beneath her fear, and Thor was almost afraid to ask. Was she mourning the loss of Jack? Did she want the man to court her sweetly?

Did she want him instead of Thor? Even after everything he'd done.

Fuck. His emotions were all over the place, and he didn't have any fucking clue how to calm them. He knew better than to think about such things. Nica was his. There was no denying how explosive they were together in bed. Her body sure as fuck knew who it belonged to, and yes, she'd even said so. But why did this have to be so hard?

"Angel, if you wanna take off work tonight, just tell me and I'll let Derrick know—"

"What? No. I don't want that. I think working might help me take my mind off this stuff," she said and nodded her head.

Pride infused him and he grinned at her, so strong and brave. Did she even know it? Could she even see the changes in her already? She wasn't meek anymore. Not scared or battered. Nica was growing into her confidence, and it was sexy as fuck.

Her soft curls felt nice under his hand, and he tried his best not to get her all mussed. It was super fucking hard, kind of like his cock, which was crazy and thoughtless cause in that moment she needed tenderness, not a rutting animal. He wanted to be the one to give her everything she needed.

"I just need you, Thor. Only you," she murmured,

tilting her head up and kissing him with impossibly soft lips.

Had he spoken aloud? Thor didn't think so, but he wasn't worrying about it since Nica was still kissing him, giving him everything he ever wanted and more. He really should stop since he could hear folks pulling up, getting ready for a night on the town. Serious Moonlight was the talk of the town, and every weekend they were jampacked with people, supes and normals alike.

Sheila had introduced these "theme nights" to interest newcomers who might think Serious Moonlight was just a place for brawling bastard MCs, and so far, it was working. Of course, a lot of her themes had to do with scantily clad women showing off their assets and bringing in the crowds, though to be fair, some of the guys got in on it, too.

In fact, he was pretty damn sure he'd seen Weylin saunter off to the bar in nothing but a Speedo and a pair of motorcycle boots. Sheila knew better than to ask Thor to participate. He'd rather die than be caught dead, tending bar in a pair of skintight underwear—*wait a second.*

"Did you buy this today?" he asked, fingering the strap of the teeny tiny bikini top he was only just noticing.

Nica blushed prettily, easing out of his embrace, and looking down as if she was unsure of herself. Fuck no. Thor was having none of that. He never wanted to break his woman down. Not ever.

"Is it all right?" she asked, biting her bottom lip in that way she had, making him wild with desire.

"All right? Angel, you look good enough to eat," he growled and leaned down to kiss her again, fast, and hard.

The soft purplish material was barely big enough to cover her ample bosoms, and his Demon Wolf snarled at the idea of anyone other than him seeing her in the tantalizing little outfit. But he wrestled with his beast, reminding him she was already claimed with his bite, his and no one else's. That helped. A little.

"All right, now that's enough of that. I can't be bouncing with a boner all night," he muttered, adjusting his steel dick in his jeans.

"Ha!"

Nica covered her mouth to hide her laugh, but he liked it too much to let her do that. Thor gently pulled her hand away and kissed her giggling lips again. He just couldn't help himself.

"Ha, nothing, you little minx. You do this to me all damn day," he confessed.

"I do?"

"Hell yes, angel. You look good enough to eat. And I will, later," he promised with a wink. "Now, if you get into trouble behind the bar tonight, just call out and I will be there fast as thunder," he told her, dropping one more kiss on her lips as they eased inside the roadhouse.

"Of course," she replied, smiling up at him.

Gods, she was pretty. All soft skin, blue eyes, pink lips, and curly dark hair. And she was his. That was the part that really got him. Nica was really his, and he was hers. He felt the truth of that down to his soul.

Mine. Mine. MINE.

But there was still a sense of foreboding plaguing him. An unease that started in the pit of his stomach. It made him want to pick her up, toss her over his shoulder, and hide her away from the whole damn world. She smiled at him again as they walked back to the bar, and he knew he could never do such a thing.

His little Raven deserved to be in the light, and he was going to make sure she had the chance to shine. That was his vow, and he swore it aloud in the old language once she was tucked away safely behind the bar with a half-naked Weylin on one side and Cole sporting a cut off wetsuit on the other.

"What in the fuck are you wearing?" he asked the long-haired Dire-Wolf, not even bothering to check Weylin's sanity.

"Sheila said I had to take part in tonight's theme, or else she was gonna slash my tires," Cole grunted.

"Damn, that's cold," Thor replied, knowing the she-Wolf meant business if she was threatening to maim a man's bike.

"You still aren't in compliance," Weylin added, butting in as usual.

"Who asked you, Mr. Banana Hammock?" Cole said, wincing at the bright yellow Speedo Weylin was wearing.

"First off, this is not a banana hammock. That term refers to a thong, which, as you can see, I am not wearing. My buttocks are perfectly covered," Weylin replied, spinning around like a fucking ballerina to show his covered assets.

"Ohmyfuckingods," Cole growled, but Weylin continued unabashed.

"Second, this is a certified Speedo, name brand, and my lady love bought me this for our trip to Hawaii we are taking next month in honor of our mating. Now, don't you all be jealous cause you can't fill this bad boy out like I can," the redhead added, waggling his eyebrows for effect.

"You wanna hit him, or should I?" Cole asked.

The dour-faced Dire Wolf Shifter had leaned back against the bar nonchalantly. With his arms crossed over his chest but Thor knew he was 100% serious in his question.

"Nah. We can get him later," Thor told him with a sharp nod.

"Okay. Then we'll have a couple of beers."

"Sounds good."

"Hey, is that nice? Is that fair? You guys wanna bond over beers and beating me up? What kind of Pack are you?" Weylin asked, running after Cole.

Thor just shook his head and walked back to his post near the front door, grateful as fuck Sheila did not bother to threaten or demand he follow any of her nutty rules about themes. His eyes found Nica adding longnecks to one of the coolers behind the bar, and the Demon Wolf inside him rumbled at the sight of her.

Now, she looked good for tonight's bikini theme in all that curve-hugging denim and the pretty little bikini top she had on. The other females had on similar ones in different colors, and he guessed they all did some shopping after their spa day. Good for them, he mused with a wide grin.

Now, Weylin, on the other hand, looked like a nut job in his lemon yellow Speedo. Come to think of it, so did Cole in his giant wetsuit onesie, even if he cut off the sleeves and the pants at the knees. It would be a cold day in hell before Thor would be caught in either outfit. He was perfectly comfortable in his usual jeans and black t-shirt, *fuck you very much*.

CHAPTER 13

Derrick had the night off. Lucky Wolf. He and Lucy were back at the Pack House with their triplets, which meant Brock was in charge. The Pack Beta and head chef was in the kitchen, making sure everything was set up perfectly for the tremendous dinner rush they often saw. Gwen was enjoying the night off, along with Phoenix's mate, Tracey. That left Thor, Nica, Weylin, Cole, Phoenix, and Sheila running the roadhouse.

Once eight o'clock rolled around, people started turning up by the dozens, and there was a pretty healthy line to get in. Thor was working the door, checking IDs, keeping the peace. It was just business as usual. An all-female band of Witches was playing tonight, more of that country rock mix the crowd seemed to like. They were good, but he wasn't much of a judge.

"Hey there, sexy. Can I rub your head for luck?".

The question caught Thor off guard. He frowned, but quickly moved out of the way of the bright pink, acrylic tipped nails the strange woman was reaching for him with. She was wearing a sparkly pink bikini over her spray tanned body and a tiny black skirt. It was possible she was a regular, but he did not recall having seen her. Her companions, either.

"Sorry, ma'am. I have a girlfriend—"

"So? What's that to me, big guy? Besides, she can't do what I can do," the woman purred.

"Sorry, letting other women touch me is a hard no. Best keep your hands to yourself. Have a good night, ladies," he told the forceful woman.

Her eyes flashed gold, and Thor sniffed. She was a Lioness. But no one he knew from the neighboring Blue Valley Pride. The she-Cat and her friends all appeared shocked that he'd said no. But whatever.

He knew their type. They were entitled and spoiled, treated like princesses by the males in their Pride who chased them. Everything about them screamed overdone, and though it was not to his liking, Thor normally didn't have an opinion on how anyone dressed or spoke. Still didn't.

In fact, he remained uncaring of the trio of females who sat nearby and kept giving him long glances that he'd successfully ignored up until Nica came over.

"Hey, I'm on break and I thought you might like a glass of iced water," she said, smiling sweetly at him.

She was so gorgeous with her bright eyes and freshly scrubbed face. He liked she didn't wear any makeup. Liked that he could see the real her all the time and didn't have to dig to find it. Everything about her was so open and freely given. He was one lucky Wolf, and he knew it. Thor took a long pull of the icy water and leaned down to nuzzle Nica's cheek affectionately.

"Thanks, angel. I was parched," he said, one big hand resting on her warm, soft waist. "You didn't have to bring this all the way over, though."

"Oh, that's okay. Weylin is watching my spot, and I wanted to see you. I missed you," she confessed, blushing prettily.

"Is that right? I've been missing you, too. Been standing here, thinking about everything I intend to do to you when we get back home," he replied, touched by her thoughtfulness, aroused by her nearness.

It got to the point where he could not stop his

dick from rising at the slightest touch from the woman, even if he tried. She wasn't just a Shifter. Nica was pure magic. And he was falling harder and faster with every second that ticked by.

"Thor, you shouldn't say things like that out loud," she whispered, clearly scandalized.

He had to kiss her again, he couldn't help himself. So he did. Quickly. He wouldn't jump on her in public or anything. Hell, his Demon Wolf was likely to kill one of these assholes if they even caught a glimpse of her wild and moaning in passion. He was too damn possessive to allow that.

Mine.

She deserved better. He knew that, but nothing could ever make him leave her now. His Nica was everything. A natural caretaker, and he had the feeling she was a secret badass, too. Warm, open, and giving, but also beautiful, fierce, and loyal. She was an ideal mate.

And Thor was so grateful he'd been there that day to catch her. He never expected to be on the receiving end of such tenderness. It felt good. She felt good. Hell, the woman was taking up so much space inside him, he could not even imagine life without her. She'd only be there for a few weeks, and in his bed for just days, and she was that deeply ingrained. He needed to tell her how he felt. That he wanted her forever, and that he loved her, even if it was too soon. He was just about to confess it all when the shit hit the fan.

"This is why you wouldn't let me touch your head? Are you serious? She's fat and plain. I mean, damn girl, maybe you should invest in some makeup if you want to keep your man," the hoity toity Lioness came stomping over on her spindly heels, interrupting Thor, and Nica.

Anger rose swiftly and Thor growled a warning, ready to defend his woman to this pissed off predator. But there was no need. Nica put her hand on his arm and turned to face the slightly tipsy female with a concerned expression on her beautiful face.

"Hi, I'm Nica. What's your name?"

"Are you kidding? You wanna know my name now, fatty? Like we are besties or something?"

"Right," Nica replied with a bashful sort of grin as she faced the woman and her friends. "Well, I don't know you, but this is the second time that I am telling you my name is Nica. Not *fatty* or *damn girl*. Just Nica. And wow, I have to say your makeup looks really good, professional even. You're lucky, you see, I have serious allergies to cosmetics, and I can't wear them at all. Lucky for me, I found a man who doesn't seem to mind," she went on, friendly as ever, facing down a trio of Lionesses, who could probably each swallow her Raven with one gulp.

Not fucking likely, his Demon Wolf snarled.

"You're allergic to makeup? Ohmygah, that sounds terrible," one of the woman's friends said.

"Yep. That's me. Allergic to makeup. But wow, I mean look at all you, so thin and trendy. Made up to the nines, and just killing those bikinis," Nica said, nodding.

"Oh, um, thanks," the original aggressor muttered, and she looked as confused as Thor.

"You really do look good tonight, ladies. Did you get those from *Gladys' Swimwear & Care* in town?"

"Oh, um, yeah. That's my aunt's shop," one of the women added.

"Nice. That's where I picked this one up, and I am lucky she carried plus sizes cause these boobs would never fit into a bikini if she didn't."

"You got great boobs," the third Lioness commented.

"Yeah, are they real?" the second one asked, and reached out to cup Nica's left breast.

"Oooh! Y-yep, thanks, they are, *um*, real," his mate stuttered, and removed the woman's hand with an awkward pat.

"Delia, what the hell? Anyway, she is right. Your boobs are great. I mean, I'm so flat, and um, I am sorry she said you were fat. You are just super curvy like a pinup model! I mean, you look really great," the first Lioness, the one who'd tried to grab Thor, told Nica.

Thor frowned. Was this woman hitting on his mate? She had a point about Nica being curvy and having great boobs, but he was not exactly comfortable with the staring or the grabbing.

Grrrr.

Nica pressed back into him, as if she knew her touch would soothe his beast. He put his arms around her waist and pulled her back against his chest. Still, she kept the conversation going with the Lionesses as if he wasn't there, growling behind her.

"Well, thank you," Nica replied honestly. "That means a super lot to me. I never had many female friends growing up, but I always wanted them, and you girls are so lucky to have each other."

"OMG! You are so sweet," one of the blonde Lionesses gushed.

"I don't know about that," Nica replied. "But, I am sure you won't have any trouble picking up men of your own if you want that, and if not, I know you will still have an awesome time tonight just doing your thing. This big guy here, though, is totally off limits. And I know that makes me super lucky. But I also know you all got more self-respect than to try flirting with a man who's spoken for, right?" Nica continued, her smile big and her blue eyes sparkling.

"You're totally right. I am sorry about all the cattiness, Nica. My name is Cheryl. This is Taylor and Delia. Anyway, thanks for being so nice about this," Cheryl told her sheepishly.

"No worries. Now, when you go to the bar, see the guy in the wetsuit? Tell him Nica said to give you a round on me," she finished and waved them away.

Thor stood there in total shock. How the fuck did she do that? The woman had to be magic or something. She had single-handedly turned a group of hostile Lionesses into sympathetic allies in just minutes with that sweet, open way she had about her. She never raised her voice or lashed out. She took their insults and turned them around, complimenting them and making them see the error of their ways as if it were their own discovery.

She was good. Really fucking good. Like pure gold. Pride zipped through his body, filling his veins as he watched her wave them off.

"Ooh, I think I better go help Weylin, he is getting slammed," she said, about to run away.

But Thor pulled her back, catching her questioning smile with his lips as he kissed the hell out of her. Yeah, his jeans were going to be really uncomfortable for a little While, but it was worth it. This woman owned him. Body, heart, mind, and soul, he belonged to her now. She had the fealty of his Demon Wolf—*gods, help them both.*

"What was that for?" she asked breathlessly when he finally came up for air.

"For being you. What you just did? Turning that volatile situation around without violence or resorting to threats? I never saw anything like that. That was fucking awesome, angel. I am so proud of you," he growled.

"I don't know, I mean, I am the lucky one, right? I have you," she said, but it sounded more like a question than a statement.

"You have me, angel. One hundred percent." He kissed her hard before swatting her on the butt so she could get back to work.

Hours later...

"Shit. I'm so tired the bags under my eyes got bags," Weylin moaned, trudging across the lot to the cottage he shared with his mate.

It had been a busy night. Seemed like people really enjoyed the bikini theme, even if Thor had to turn away a couple of enthusiasts who insisted dental floss was acceptable attire.

"Was it mint?"

"What?" he asked Nica, who'd been quiet to that point.

"The dental floss," she said, brows furrowed.

"Nica, I didn't say any of that out loud."

"You didn't?"

Thor shook his head. His mate stopped and turned to face him, her whole expression one of abject confusion. The crisp Autumn air swirled around them, and the sounds of dried leaves rustling was a soft hum in the background. Nica's heart was pounding, and his own matched its pace. He felt like the very air was charged with something *other*.

"I think it's because of our matebond," he murmured.

"Matebond? What is that?"

Thor's Demon Wolf stirred, the animal wanting to be with his mate. Inside his mind's eye, Thor saw the thin strands of their new matebond. It was warm and gold and pulsed as he drew near. His beast staring off into the ether, as if he was waiting for something.

Yes. Waiting. Always waiting.

CHAPTER 14

Thor stood on the periphery of the forest with his eyes closed, and Nica knew he was attempting to communicate with the Wolf inside him. Her own beast stirred. The sound of her thick, shaggy feathers rustling filled the inside of her mind's eye, and Nica doubled over. She felt sick with the need to shift.

Not safe. Not safe.

But telling her Raven it was not safe to change didn't seem to do the trick as it had over the past few weeks. Her stomach cramped, and she whimpered. Trying to fight a shift sucked. It was painful in a way she could hardly describe. Like a million tiny needles pricking all over her body, while her gut was twisted, clenched inside a giant vise.

"Nica!" Thor rushed to her, his black eyes glittering at her in the darkness.

"Can't let her out," she grunted.

"How long has it been?" he asked, and panic hit her.

He knew her secret. Knew she'd been too afraid to change. For some reason, she felt so ashamed. He deserved a better mate. Someone who was strong enough to get out of a bad situation before it got to the point of no return. Someone who wasn't afraid of themselves like she was. Tears filled her eyes, and she moaned, falling to her knees. Then he was there, lifting her in his arms and cupping her face, asking her again.

"How long you been keeping her locked up, angel?"

"Since the day I fell, and you caught me," she replied and saw the horror in his gaze.

He would think she was a coward now, for sure. Sadness filled her at the thought of disappointing him, but Thor merely shook his head. He looked determined and powerful. She saw the mists swirling around him again, and the frank proof he was strong, that he was other was like a wake up call. Thor was magnificent, and at the very least, she could try to be brave for him.

"You're safe here. You can Shift here with me," he growled, his response brooked no arguments.

"I can't. The Crows are watching me, I know they are, and Thor, I never want to go back," she told him with feeling.

"You can do this, and I promise you will never go back there," he said, still cupping her cheeks with his hands and kissing her head.

"Look, let me explain, angel."

Thor stood up and pulled her to her feet. He took her hand, his big one swallowed hers, but she never felt as safe as she did with him. He walked her into the forest behind the parking lot. It ran the length of the property, but Nica had never ventured into the woods before. She had no reason to.

"The forest is ours from just beyond the creek to the property here where the bar, the Pack House, and the smaller houses all sit. This land is the property of the Dire Wolf MC, and any trespassers would violate our claims to this territory. We don't fall under the purview of the Shifter Council, but we have a longstanding treaty with them."

"What does that mean?" she asked.

It was good to know, but she didn't understand what it had to do with her very real fear that if she shifted and flew, the Murder would swoop in and attack like the sneaky bastards they were. She frowned, watching Thor as he shook his head, those dark eyes glittering with something that looked a whole lot like mischief and maybe some pride.

She'd seen the man angry, annoyed, serious, and horny, but his teasing face was the one that got her in the gut every single time. Gods, he was gorgeous. Spending the last two days wrapped around each other must have cut into his shaving time, because the two-day-old bristle on his face and head was darker than ever. Nica liked it. A lot. There was something dangerous about a man who looked better the scruffier he got.

"What it means is you can change here any fucking time you want, angel. The same laws that Crow motherfucker is trying to use against us will protect you. I will protect you," he told her with a wicked grin and a promise in his eyes that settled something inside her.

Her Raven cawed. The animal was tired of being cooped up. She was weaker, unused to being kept from the world. And there as something else, too. She wanted to meet her mate in her feathers, not just her human skin. She needed to connect with him like that.

"Is that what you were talking out with those two

men earlier? The twins?"

"The Lowell brothers? Yeah. Those Wolves are lawyers for the Macconwood Pack. They're the largest Wolf Pack in North America. You see, he didn't wait for us to get back to him. Jack Branwen went right to the Shifter Council of New Jersey and filed a formal complaint," he told her in a rush.

"Wait. He challenged you?" she asked, wide eyed.

"Fuck no. He's too much of a pussy to challenge me. He is making a claim that by Crow law, you are his mate because of the promising ceremony your mother signed off on. But the Lowell boys said it doesn't hold water. That law is outdated, plus with the increase in female Shifters on the Council, there is no way in hell they'd vote for you to return to a mate you didn't pick. And even if they did, I already bit you, Nica. You are mine. Anyone who says differently can kiss my big ass," he growled.

"So, you were busy working this out, looking for ways to take care of me while I was getting massaged and waxed?" Nica laughed, not realizing tears had fallen from her eyes until he wiped them away.

"Who the fuck gave you a massage, angel?" he growled, but she giggled in response.

"A Witch named Helga at the spa we went to in

town. She gave me a bikini wax, too. You want one? I can book her for you," Nica teased.

"Bikini wax?" he murmured, eyebrows high as he mentally pictured what she was saying.

Then he shook his head abruptly, as if he had just processed the rest of what she'd asked him. Nica couldn't stifle her laugh if she tried.

"Hell no, I don't want one. Only woman I want touching me is you," Thor stated, kissing her hungrily, and making her knees weak.

"Good."

"Good, huh? Possessive little thing, aren't you?"

"Sorry," she began, frowning.

"Don't be sorry. I like it. I'm the same way about you."

"You are?"

"Yep. Look, this is big between us, angel. Big and good. I feel it in here," he growled, rubbing his chest.

His focus was so intent on her, Nica's knees knocked. She swallowed hard, unsure of how to respond. Yes, she felt it, but she couldn't just say it. Could she? Her Raven cawed, and the air grew heavy and shimmery, making her shiver. Then Thor just switched it off, his eyes cleared, and he grinned, lightening the mood.

"Come on, I swear this will be fun. Oh, I want to

tell you something else, too," he started, heading towards a gigantic oak tree that still had its leaves.

The entire forest was awash in Autumn colors. Greens had given way to reds, golds, purples, and oranges. It was like a painting in a magazine she'd once seen a long time ago. The colors were like a riotous symphony dancing on the early morning breeze. It had to be near four o'clock already, tonight being one of the latter nights that the bar stayed open.

"What did you want to tell me?" she whispered the question.

It felt right to whisper. Awed by all the beauty surrounding them, she turned her eyes back to Thor's and felt his gaze like hands brushing across her skin with nothing less than wonder. He touched her gently, caressing her face as he spoke, turning her insides to mush.

"The thing is, I think our matebond needs help. You know that telepathic link we have sometimes? It isn't truly formed. It's weak, always coming and going, and I believe it is because you haven't changed in so long. Our animals haven't had a chance to sync yet, and it's messing with our connection."

"Oh, I see. That's why I can only hear you sometimes in my head," she whispered, nodding her understanding. "I'm so sorry, I didn't think."

"Don't apologize, angel. You have nothing to be sorry for," he said, kissing her knuckles.

"Do you really think it's safe to shift here?"

"Yes. The Crows have been given strict rules to stay off Dire Wolf lands. As long as you don't go past our boundaries, you will be fine. I'll show you where those are."

"All right, I trust you," she said, and Thor seemed to light up like the fourth of July.

"Gimme a sec to make sure no one else is here," he said, stilling her hand when she went to unbutton her jeans.

Nica's cheeks flamed pink with embarrassment and Thor just swung an arm around her and chuckled deeply. Dang, she loved that sound. She had a feeling the big man didn't laugh very often, and it warmed her to her soul.

Thor let out two sharp barks and whatever stragglers were about, Pack or not, she was sure they skedaddled. It was definitely not a typical response that she thought he was hot for basically threatening to maim anyone who saw her naked body. But whatever. They were Shifters, not normals, so that was okay.

Mine, the word whispered inside her mind, and Nica shivered with delight.

"Yours," she repeated aloud, pressing into his side.

With every step closer to the forest and to her first change in weeks, Nica felt their matebond growing stronger, thicker, more powerful. Her Raven flapped her wings, eager to be let out. Her senses felt heightened and that something else about her, the one that sometimes let her see more than she ought to, was vibrant and alert.

She turned her gaze to Thor, and what she saw stole her breath. The man was magic. Pure magic. His whole body seemed awash in glittery black smoke, swirling and dancing around him like those ribbons on a stick she used to play with when she was little. He was magnificent, and Nica was so grateful he was hers.

After he made certain they were alone, Thor nodded his head, giving her the okay to strip out of her clothes. Oh, sure, she'd had all sorts of fantasies about him taking the little bikini she wore, with his teeth preferably, but this was important. Maybe they could get to all that afterwards.

I hope so.

"Don't worry. You can always put it back on later," he murmured, and her cheeks burned under his knowing stare.

"You're reading my mind again," she murmured, mouth going dry as she watched him shuck off his jeans and his t-shirt.

"Was I reading your mind?"

"Yeah, you were," he said, raking her with his eyes from head to toe.

He got to her clothes next. Thor was careful, gentle, brushing across her sensitive skin with his fingertips and knuckles. She never knew a man's hands could be so damn beautiful, but his were. Strong and solid, with long fingers and intricate tattoos across the backs. There were Wolves and a beautiful rendition of a forest with a full moon hanging overhead.

Nica squinted, thinking she saw a bird sitting in a tree, a raven, actually. But then he touched her again, and she lost her train of thought. By the time he was finished, she could hardly speak. Need pulsed through her veins, a living thing, and Nica swayed towards him unsteadily.

Need. Want.

He made her feel like a goddess when he looked

at her and touched her so carefully. Thor was the only man who ever made her come completely undone with just his eyes. Hell, any second now, she was going to drop to the floor to worship at his feet.

Maybe she would. After she shifted, though. Not before.

CHAPTER 15

Thor's heart raced inside his chest as he undressed his gorgeous mate. It was early morning hours and all he wanted was to get her back to their room, strip her naked and make her come a time or ten before they fell into a sleep so deep it only happened when you were truly exhausted or satisfied. He was banking on the latter.

But Nica needed this. Her Raven needed this. And if he were being totally honest, his Demon Wolf did, too. The growl building in his chest told him he'd hit the nail on the head, and with one more thorough glance around, he nodded. He tucked their clothes in a neat pile on the floor and gave her one more reassuring squeeze on her shoulders before he turned her around to face the woods. Fuck, the view was even better from behind. Thor's cock throbbed, jutting out from between his legs, letting all and sundry know just how badly he wanted her.

Later, he promised himself. He wasn't a totally thoughtless oaf. His mate needed to feel safe and secure to change, and he would give his right arm to do that for her. She deserved to feel safe. The fact anyone had ever hurt her made his blood boil, but he stilled the growl in his throat knowing she needed this more than he needed to voice his desire for revenge.

Mine.

"Go on, Angel. I got you," he assured her.

Some Shifters had a hard time swapping skins, and Thor braced himself for whatever happened when a woman morphed into a badass bird. Her Raven was large, he recalled, but still much smaller than her human shape. He could not even fathom how it was possible.

Well, that wasn't entirely true. Thor's connection to the *other* brought him a different aspect of what was possible and what wasn't. Shifters had walked the earth longer than normals. Their origins were as deeply ingrained in the multiverse as any of the sentient creatures in the preternatural world.

Knowing all that usually brought him a certain

sense of peace, but Thor felt his hackles rise as he noted the change in her scent. She was nervous, anxious, possibly both. He frowned, but held on to his control, batting down on all his protective instincts. On a scale from one to ten, they were at an eleven.

Doubts plagued him. What if he was wrong? What if this was a bad idea? But no. How could it be?

Thor understood her animal's needs. The beast inside her needed to come out so their matebond could grow and blossom. It was a necessary step. Nica had already seen and accepted his Demon Wolf. Besides, he was right there. Thor would never allow her to get hurt. Not for the whole fucking world. Still, he had to force himself to back off. He needed to trust her to know what to do, so he bit his tongue and waited.

The air trembled around them. It started shimmering and glowing with Shifter magic he could see as clear as day. Oh, but it was beautiful. Nica's Raven was black as midnight, and the magic accompanying her shift reflected that. It was all glittering black diamonds and sparkling blue fire. It danced along her skin, permeating the air with the scent of strawberry jam, fresh baked bread, and ozone.

He looked on helplessly, mesmerized, as her

human shape began to transform. Limbs morphed, bones broke, and muscles reshaped. Nica didn't shudder or cry as some Shifters did when changing. Instead, she just fell into her other shape with the softest of sighs, like when she was kissing him. One minute she was on two legs, the next she was covered in glossy black, shaggy feathers that extended down to the center of her pointed beak.

Gods, she was beautiful. So much so, she stole the breath from his body. He coveted her with his hungry gaze, wanting her more than anything. But with that wanting came a bone deep tenderness. Once acknowledged, that feeling was so profound, Thor dropped to his knees at her talons right there in the middle of the forest.

"Are you all right, mate?"

Her sweet voice filled his head, and Thor closed his eyes to stave off a wave of dizziness. Oh, he'd heard her before, he realized, but never this clear or loud. Their matebond pulsed around them and when he looked down, he saw it. Their bond was beautiful, ethereal, full of color and magic.

It connected them, tethered them together like a long, fettered rope. If he didn't think she was fated to be his before, he damn well knew it now. Possessiveness, love, and devotion surged inside him. And something more, a need he had never felt before.

Like he wanted to bare his soul to her. Dangerous. She was dangerous. Chipping away at the carefully laid walls he'd placed around his heart to stop anyone getting too close. Nica did all that and more. She made him want to be better. She made him want to try harder.

But there were parts of him that were so dark, so full of fear and rage. Sometimes, when he went past the veil, Thor didn't think he would make it back, and that was the biggest fear he had. He frowned hard, wondering how to explain, if he should explain. He wasn't certain someone filled with such a bright light would understand.

Despite that, Thor still wanted to show her all the grit and dirt that clung to him. He wanted to confess those secrets that were so damn ugly about him, just to see if she still loved him. And she loved him, all right. Just like he loved her. Neither of them had said it yet, but he felt it, especially with her in this shape.

Caw caw.

Her Raven's call brought him back to the present. Thor wiped a hand over his face, forgetting his worries as he simply took her in. She canted her head, black eyes flashing at him, and he grinned.

"Fuck, Nica, you are so gorgeous in your feathers. Wanna run with you, angel."

"Let's go then."

Her reply was short and sweet, and he could hear the smile in her voice. No sooner had she agreed than Thor was swapping his own skin for fur. His change was swift, instantaneous. In the blink of an eye, Thor's human body swapped places with his Wolf. He shook his enormous body hard, chasing away any leftover tingles.

Nica had been right about calling his Demon Wolf brindled, though he hardly gave it a thought. His fur was dark at the roots, like an almost black espresso brown that lightened to pure gold at the tips. His muzzle was the same black brown as his roots, but it was his eyes that usually frightened people. Thor's Wolf's eyes were pure black, holding no white at all.

He was also monstrously huge, of course, like the other Dire Wolves. But Nica had already met his beast, so he knew she would not falter at the sight of him. On the contrary, his sassy little Raven hopped up on his back, ruffling him with her beak behind his ears before cawing and taking off into the sky.

She flew low, dodging trees, and scaring the shit out of him, but Thor kept pace easily. He could feel her happiness, and he loved it. It was addictive, and he was already planning their next adventure like this. Yeah, he would go running with her flying overhead daily if she wanted to. She was something, alright. A true wonder in his Wolf's eyes.

Hours later they fell back into their skin beside the creek, and yeah, it was *hella* cold, but that didn't stop him from picking her up and jumping in the frigid water with her. Just having her curvy, warm body in his arms was worth it.

"Thor!" she squealed, clutching his shoulders when they hit the water.

He kissed her before she could protest again. Like so many of their kisses, it grew hot and heavy in a matter of seconds. She was perfect like this, submissive and aggressive all at the same time. She seemed to know exactly when to demand, and when to give in, writhing her sexy little body all over him, and driving him out of his damned mind.

Before he knew it, Thor was already pressing into her tight heat with her back up against the flat side of a bolder in the shallow side of the waters. Fuck, her pussy felt like heaven. Hot, wet, tight heaven. She clenched around him, sending lightning bolts of pleasure shooting through his veins. He was an animal taking her rough like this, but he couldn't help it. He needed her like he needed air. Maybe more.

Fuck yes, more.

"Mine," he grunted, pushing his hips harder, faster, stroking her walls just right. "Tell me," he commanded, needing to hear it.

"Yours, Thor. I'm yours," she repeated over and over aloud and in her thoughts, pushing the words right into his head.

Hearing her voice in his head was fucking magic. A kind of magic he never thought he would share with anyone, but Nica was not just anyone. She was his heart and soul.

"Harder," she moaned, and he obliged, pounding into her sweet sex until he almost blew without her.

"Need you to come for me, angel. Now, right now," he demanded, and miracle of miracles, she did.

Nica clawed his back like the little hellion she was, crying out his name. There was nothing sexier on the whole fucking planet than his mate's face when she came all over him. Thor roared in ecstasy, her pussy clamping down on his dick right before he exploded into his own spiral of pleasure.

Warm jets shot into her, a direct contrast to the

cold water surrounding them, and he could hardly catch his breath. He'd never felt anything so intense. The air shimmered, the veil between worlds and planes disrupting around him as he came and came and came some more inside of his mate.

My mate. My fated one. My one and only.

He didn't deserve her, but he would do everything he could to be worthy. She was precious to him now. Ingrained in his very soul, and branded on his heart. Oh, she had his loyalty. His Demon Wolf's too.

Thor was never going to give her up. Not ever. He was going to love her for the rest of his life, and several lifetimes after that. He closed his eyes, feeling his ancestors cheering him on, offering congratulations, and blessing their union. It was phenomenal. Important. And so damn big, he could hardly think of any words to explain it.

Eons later he felt soft kisses on his face, and his shaved head as Nica tended him, whispering sweetly.

"I got you, mate. I got you."

She did. Heart, body, mind, and soul. Nica had him all right. Thor closed his eyes to slow his pounding heart and, doing so, he saw his Demon Wolf. The animal sat and watched her with hungry eyes in that metaphysical plane where he existed till called, and he wasn't alone. His Raven mate sat with him and their matebond glowed between them, ten times as thick as before.

"I got you too, angel."

And he meant it. He really did.

CHAPTER 16

The days sped by in blissful happiness. Those turned into weeks with no word from the Murder or the Shifter Council. Nica was too busy enjoying every moment to give it much more than a passing thought.

She was busy building a life. Days were spent working in the bar, helping with the triplets, and doing chores in the Pack House. It was fall, but that didn't stop Thor from building her a miniature greenhouse in the back. She had been so touched by his efforts, her heart almost exploded when she saw what he was doing.

The others all pitched in, and when the outside construction was done, he'd furnished worktables and shelves, set up the plumbing, and went with her to a huge garden center to place an order for things she'd need.

"Are you sure about all this? It's expensive," she'd said, worrying.

"Of course, I'm sure. I think we should stop by the community college to get some course pamphlets for next semester, see if they have the kind of classes you were taking before."

"Really? You would do that for me?"

"I'd do anything for you," he said, his expression so serious it bordered on bafflement.

True, Nica was a homey sort, and didn't mind housework or any work. But this touched her deeply. Thor listened to her, and if she was not already head over heels in love with the man, that right there would have done it. He was still protective, always worried about others taking advantage of her work ethic. He didn't want her doing too much.

"You don't have to do the dishes tonight, angel," he told her after dinner one evening.

"I know, but I don't mind."

"Here, lemme get 'em. You go sit and enjoy your coffee."

She was still stunned a man like that would do

things like the dishes, taking out the trash, and carrying the shopping. But he did things like that often. And not in any *me strong man, you feeble woman* sort of way. Thor was a natural born provider. A soul deep protector, but he had a sweet side, too. She was just lucky and totally happy his gentle side only came out for her.

She'd just finished unboxing an order she'd placed for gloves, hand trowels, sheers, and other gardening tools inside the greenhouse. Next week, she would get her first shipment of soil and seeds. Thor was still working on the heated lights they would need to ensure the seedlings and plants did not freeze during the winter. Once that was finished, he was going to help her build some hydroponic planters. Nica had all sorts of ideas about how to combine hydroponics with traditional gardening to grow things faster and bigger than ever.

For the first time in her life, Nica was truly happy. It was addicting and contagious, she realized, thinking about how much more Thor seemed to smile now. Their days were amazing, but their nights were even better.

It was nothing short of ecstasy, spending each night wrapped up in the man she'd come to love and worship with every inch of herself. Gods, the man was insatiable, and thank goodness, so was she. Thor brought out a side of her she never even knew she had. He might not be demanding in any other aspect of their relationship, but in bed, Thor was the master.

He'd introduced her to more carnal delights, more sensual pleasures than she ever realized existed. Sex was important to Shifters, to everyone, she supposed. When Thor was buried deep inside her, demanding she tell him who she belonged to, well, that was Nica's favorite thing. She loved the way he made her spiral, the way he pushed her higher and higher, demanding more than anyone ever had, and yes, she complied with those demands willingly, desperately even.

Every. Single. Night.

"Tell me you're mine, angel."

"Yes, yes, I am yours. Always. Only yours. Yours. YOURS."

Her body hummed even now with remembered pleasure, and she smiled as she pictured the things he'd said and done to her just hours ago that very morning. Oh yes. No doubt about it. Thor was a dream of a mate. Gorgeous, physically perfect, kind, funny, smart, sweet, with a direct approach that left her gasping.

He paid her so much attention, and he listened to her when she spoke. He offered his opinion, but never forced it. She didn't know a mate could be like that. That men, in general, could be fair-minded and tender with their women. Back in the Murder, the males were like tyrants, dictating what the females should be doing and when.

There were only about half a dozen of them. But a more beaten group of women, Nica had never seen. So different from the females of the Dire Wolf Pack. Even Ella and Denise, who had been kind to her at first, taking her in and helping her adjust to Jack's way of doing things, had changed the way they felt about her the moment they realized she was there to join their ranks as just another mate to the Crow King. Her naïve notions of romance were very short-lived back then. Reality in the Murder was a dream killer.

She'd been so pitifully green, wearing rose-tinted glasses when she looked at the world, so unaware of how badly Jack had abused her trust and innocence. But Nica was not the only one who'd suffered because of his lies. Jack wasn't a heartbreaker in that cute boy cocky sense people often joked about. He was literally a heartbreaker, in that he tore the love right out of a person, leaving them bereft, gutted and hopeless.

"You think you can come here with your young ass and take him from us? Jack is ours! You're just a little slut. He thinks he needs you to get himself an heir, but I got that handled. Don't you worry about it, missy. Just keep your head down and when Jack comes calling, you say no!" Denise had seethed.

It broke Nica's heart to see the tears in the older woman's eyes hidden behind her rage and cruelty. That was part of Nica's curse, though, seeing deeper than most. She only wished she'd seen the truth in Jack's eyes before she'd gone with him all those years ago. But no. she would not regret the past or her decisions. After all, those had led her here, to her true mate.

Thor. My Thor.

Her Raven cawed, the animal as crazy about the man as her human side was. Speaking of the man, he ambled over to her, wiping his hands on the back of his jeans. She saw the smear of grease and grinned.

He'd been working on his bike while she'd been unpacking her boxes. He wanted to get it ready so he could take her for a ride. It'd taken days of begging, but finally, he'd given in. Good mate that he was, Thor insisted on making sure his motorcycle was in top shape before putting her on the back. As if it would be anything but, she mused.

He was meticulous with all his possessions. Careful and precise in his handling of them, including Nica. She supposed it was antifeminist to think of herself as belonging to Thor, but that was just one opinion.

She found belonging to someone was more liberating than she ever expected. Belonging to Thor was a dream come true. Gods, she loved the man. She still hadn't told him yet. Not in those words, but she tried to show him every single day.

"Come here, angel," he growled, his bold gaze raking her from head to toe.

Nica went readily, loving the way he seemed to always want her. It felt so good. It felt so right. After all, she was of the same mind. He kissed her eagerly, with a barely restrained hunger, sending waves of need rippling through her body. She moaned her desire right back at him. Sometimes Nica didn't know what to do with all that stark intensity and masculinity. She returned his desire, was desperate to get closer to him. Nica only hoped it was enough for him. *She* wanted to be enough for him.

"You know you are, angel," he told her, reading

her thoughts now that their bond was stronger than ever.

"It's weird with you being in my head all the time," she murmured, clinging to him as he slowed their kiss.

Thor stilled, and when she looked up, it was to see him frowning at her. Nica swallowed. Dang. She hated her insecurities were so open to him, but she didn't want to make him upset, but this was all so new to her. Still, she bit her lower lip and waited for his reaction.

"Do you not like it? I can try to shut it off some of the time at least," he replied, rubbing his head thoughtfully.

"Oh, I'm not trying to shut you out or anything," she blurted, one part relieved he was not mad, and the other part worried he might think she didn't want him.

"No, yeah, I know," he mumbled, not very convincing either.

He also stepped away from her, which was a first. Normally, when they were apart, even for just a few hours, he couldn't stop touching her. But not this time. He moved back another inch, and it might as well have been a mile. Nica shivered, cold without his body heat. But there was another reason. She felt like he was distancing himself from her, and it hurt.

"Thor? It's just, privacy was not something I was really afforded in the Pine Murder. I like that I have the choice here to be private or to share. I do love that we can communicate without words, dang, I am doing this all wrong. I'm sorry," she said, shoulders sagging.

A long, tense moment passed while she waited for him to respond. It was impossible to gauge his reaction, and Nica was on tenterhooks.

"I hear you, angel, and I'm sorry. This is new for me too, but I'll try to respect your boundaries, okay?"

"Okay," she whispered. It was a win, for sure, but somehow, she felt like she'd lost something.

"Um, let's skip the ride, okay? I'm kind of tired. How about we just go for a quick run through the woods right here?" Thor suggested, nodding towards the place that had become like a sanctuary to her.

She followed his gaze to the trail they normally took. Thor missed the look of disappointment that flashed across her face, and she quickly schooled her features to show nothing of her disappointment. By the time his gaze landed back on her, she'd already disguised it.

"Okay. Sounds good."

He led the way into the woods and stepped back to give her some privacy to shuck her clothing. Usually, he helped her remove them, not like she needed it, but it was just something he did. Not today though, and she felt cold without his warm, large hands to heat her.

He was giving her space. Something she hadn't asked for before, and she knew it was her fault. Nica's heart squeezed inside her chest. She normally felt excited about changing into her animal with him, but the joy had been sucked out of the day by her thoughtless words.

She needed to focus on the positive. She was here, now, with her mate, and about to join him in her animal form. That he accepted her was amazing. In her limited experience, Shifters stayed with their own kind. But the Dire Wolves were different. They followed their hearts, and that was amazing.

Thor's brindled Dire Wolf was the most gorgeous creature she'd ever seen, and when she was in Raven form, her eyesight was that much keener. He was all muscle and strength, his black eyes glittering with power. She'd never seen a more dominant and majestic animal.

Nica would fix the hurt she'd caused by asking for privacy. She would mend this minor rift because she wanted to. Yes, being *matebonded* was new and kind of scary, but she was stronger than she had ever been. She was a better version of herself with him. Maybe if she explained she just needed time and care, it would be okay.

No maybe, it would be, she corrected herself.

By the time she hopped back to the lane in her feathers, croaking deep in her throat as she searched for her mate, he was already there, waiting for her in his Wolf's gorgeous brindled fur. She cawed, letting him know she was going to take to the air, but the animal stepped forward, blocking her path and Nica stilled.

Nica froze. Nerves kept her from twitching, even though she knew Thor would never harm her, even when he was wearing his magnificent beast's skin. Demon sniffed along her head and back, the nickname she'd given him felt apropos especially since she knew it meant something entirely different from the Judeo Christian definition of the word. He was the descendant of Vikings. A mighty warrior Wolf gifted by the gods to be so much more than she could have ever dreamed in this lifetime.

Demon's growl reverberated in his chest as he rubbed his lupine face against her body, marking her with his scent, letting her and everyone else know she belonged to him. He wasn't mad or disappointed. He still loved her. Nica loosed a deep, satisfied croak. Her human had hurt his earlier, but she would make it up to him.

Boundaries were tough in any relationship, but when one of them was a little bit psychic and the other a little bit sheltered, communication was highly important.

Normally, she would just send her thoughts to him in this form, but when she tried, she just couldn't. Nica cawed, but Thor simply canted his head, waiting for her to take to the skies as he usually did.

Crap. Messing up did not feel good at all. But she'd apologize and tell him how much she cared about him, and how much she wanted to grow their matebond as soon as they finished their run. She was certain now that if they just took some time to explore their bond together, she wouldn't feel so anxious about it.

Truth was, the depth of her feeling for Thor was

immeasurable. Scared the crap out of her most of the time. She was in love. Not lust. Not like. But really in love. He was so big. He felt like everything to her.

But what if he didn't want her for keeps like she wanted him? What if this was just a passing thing? Wolves mated for life, but did they still do that if their mates weren't Wolves, too?

She had so many questions. Nica wasn't educated like Thor, who had two degrees in theology and Philosophy on top of his vast world experience. She sure as heck was not on the level of beautiful as him. So, what was keeping him there?

Dang it. She hated feeling inadequate, like she didn't have the right tools for the job. The wind was coming in powerful gusts, blowing Nica to the side, and she righted herself, but it was difficult to focus when her brain was a mess of feelings. All she knew was she loved Thor, and that had to count, right?

Tell him, her Raven insisted.

Yeah. The animal was right. Nica needed to talk to him. The sooner the better. The swoosh of her wings was loud as the passing wind as she soared high above Thor. Looking down, she wished she could tell him everything she was seeing, but with their bond closed tight, she couldn't.

Oh well. It will have to wait.

Thor snarled and barked from below. She cawed a reply, but there was no way for him to understand her. Nica cursed herself for being the reason he closed their link. What was he trying to tell her?

She looked up, shrieking, when she suddenly understood what had her mate in a frenzy. The two tall pines that marked the end of the Dire Wolf territory whizzed past her. Darn it. Nica had been so damn lost in thought, she hadn't been paying attention to where she was headed.

No no no! How could I make such a big mistake?

Thor's growls and snarls grew frantic, and she tried to slow down so she could safely come around again. But before she could turn, something slammed into her from the side. Nica spun to the left, seeing stars explode behind her eyes. She tried to right herself, but she'd been flying too fast and started hurtling towards the ground. Desperate to slow down, she spread her wings as far as she could, hoping the air would slow her down in a parachute effect.

Please gods, please.

Bam! She got hit again. This time from the other side. Raven cawed in pain as something grabbed her wings and pulled. No, not something, but two pairs of somethings. The sounds of Thor's howls and snarls from down below echoed in her ears, and the realization she might never see him sent icy tendrils of fear spiking through her heart.

Caw! Caw! Caw!

The shortened caw of the Crows filled her head, and she wanted to scream her rage. It was them. The Pine Murder. Four of their Crows had been waiting for her to cross the boundary line. And now, because of her foolishness, they had her now.

Disoriented and scared out of her mind, Nica tried to fight. A viciously sharp peck from the biggest Crow, from Jack's monster bird, had blood dripping down her face. She was immobilized as their sharp talons dug into her wings, forcing them wide.

She cried out, to no avail, as they yanked her far away from the Dire Wolf Pack. Far away from *him*. Thor's howls were further away now. He was following her on the ground, but the crows flew higher and higher, zigzagging until her mate couldn't see them any longer.

The Crows knew better than to lead the Demon Wolf over the forest. Her heart broke for what she could have had as they dragged her away from the first taste of happiness she had ever known. Smarter than she gave them credit for, the Crows headed for the highway, where dozens of normals might overlook a bunch of birds, but not a monstrous Wolf.

Cursing her stupidity, she croaked one more time. A Raven's goodbye to the only man she ever loved. Who knew what Jack would do with her now? She didn't even care.

Oh gods, no. Thor, forgive me. I am so sorry. So very sorry.

CHAPTER 17

Thor raced like a madman back to the Pack House. He didn't even bother to grab clothes as he hunted Derrick down.

"Fuck Thor, put on some pants," the Alpha growled, covering his mate's eyes with his big hand.

"They took her," he growled, barely holding on to his fury.

"What?! They came on our lands?" the Alpha asked, standing up swiftly.

"No. She crossed the boundary in the woods. Fuck, it's my fault. She wanted to go for a ride on my bike, then she said something about our bond being too much and I cut it off. I was stupid and hurt, but then she was flying and I, I couldn't fucking warn her! I acted like a possessive asshole and now my mate is in the hands of the motherfucker who hurt her in the first place!"

Thor fell to his knees, holding on to his head as pain the likes of which he never felt filled him. The shadow spirits were lurking closer, then, begging him to let them in, promising to give him the vengeance he desired. He wasn't strong enough to resist them. Thor couldn't hold on to his grip on this world, his sanity, anything—*not without her*. Nica was his everything, and he'd ben to weak and proud to take care of her. He let this happen. By pushing too hard. Not talking enough. This was his fault.

"Thor? Thor! Stop! Stop it right now!"

The Alpha command snapped him out of that dark place he'd fallen into. When he focused, he saw not Derrick, but Lucy, and she was kneeling in front of him. His face stung, and from the position of her arm, he realized the tiny Alpha fem must have slapped him. Hard, too.

"Nica needs you right now. I don't give a crap what the Council said. Those Crows took her against her will. That is kidnapping. Now, are you ready to get your mate back?" she asked.

"Lucy," Derrick started, but the woman flashed a glare at her mate before turning back to Thor.

"You call the Council or the Lowell brothers or

whoever the fuck else you want, Derrick, but Nica is my friend, and I am going with her mate to get her back."

"Fuck," the Alpha snarled, then added. "But put on some fucking pants, Thor. I'm not sitting next to you with your dick hanging out, for fuck's sake."

"We are gonna get her back," Lucy reassured him, before standing up.

Thor nodded, too numb to do much else. He ran to his room, grabbed some clothes, and raced outside in jeans and his boots. He could do without the rest. Dark energy swirled around him, and Thor didn't need to look in the mirrors of his Harley to see his eyes were completely black.

He'd been trying so hard to balance his life, half in and half out of the other world, he never fully realized what that did to those around him. Anger and fury, the rage of restless spirits batted against him, but he had no time for that. Thor had one focus now.

Nica.

He revved his engine, growling in satisfaction as the sounds of his Pack mates bikes echoed his. Together, they hauled ass like bats out of hell, or Wolves on the prowl, he supposed. The Pine Murder thought they could hide behind laws, but the Dire

Wolves were a law unto themselves. They had been for eons. No shit stain Crow King was going to change that.

Jack Branwen had fucked with the wrong female. Maybe trusted his men to keep him safe. Or maybe because he hid behind petty rules, he thought they applied to everyone. Fucking scumbag. He had no idea what he was fucking with. Thor didn't care about the rules or man or beast.

He was a motherfucking Seer. He dealt with things small minds like Branwen's could not even comprehend. That asshole had riled the wrong monster. Demon Wolf was coming now. And he was angry as fuck.

———

"Oh my gods, Jack. Do you have any idea what my mate is gonna do to you when he comes for me?" Nica asked.

She laughed aloud at the pitiful man even as blood trickled down from the wound, he'd given her on her head when his Crow hit her in the sky. Dang. Her body ached, and she shivered involuntarily. Nica was bruised and sore, and her left shoulder screamed in pain. Dislocated, she knew. After all, it wasn't the first time.

"Shut up! *I* am your mate," the pathetic man screamed, pulling on his own hair as spittle flew from his mouth.

"No, you're not. You never were. Hell, Jack, you don't even know what it means to be a real mate," she told him, unflinching when he raised his hand and struck her again.

"SHUT UP!" he wailed, but Nica simply wheezed a laugh.

She was naked, cold, tied to the same hated pole he'd shackled her to all those weeks ago. But unlike last time, she didn't feel alone and scared. She knew better now.

The entire Murder was gathered around, except for poor Ella, whose passing had recently occurred. The same males who guarded the King hovered close, though none looked quite sure about what was happening. Denise was still there, eyes rimmed in red, like she'd been crying for days. Nica's gaze landed on her, and the woman doubled over, sobbing.

"Get her out of here. Useless bitch," Jack snarled, stomping over to the fallen woman, and pulling her hair. He shoved her at one of his men, who carried her away.

There were less than two dozen in the Murder now. Small numbers for a group that once boasted a hundred strong. It was his poor leadership that sent them away. Nica knew that, even if Jack still lived under the grand delusion he was a mighty King.

"Where are all your Crows, Jack? Did they leave their weak King?" she taunted.

"Weak? I stole you back, whore. I took you while your mate was stuck on the ground, powerless to stop me! Who is weak now?" he shouted, arms wide in an attempt to appear triumphant.

"Still you, Jack. You're still the weak one. I can't imagine Thor would ever have to kidnap a woman or trick her into signing some piece of paper to get her to be with him."

"Fucking bitch," he snarled, looking around for something, a weapon likely.

"What's the matter? Can't kill me with your hands?"

"You are just begging for it, Domenica. Keep testing me and I will show you exactly how strong I am. Stand her up!" he commanded.

Two Crows came forward, releasing her from the pole and pulling on her manacled hands till she stood before him. She was naked, dirty, and covered in bruised, but Nica did not care. Jack's eyes raked over her body, sending tendrils of fear and revulsion through her, but she needed to be strong.

She wanted him focused on her. Didn't care about his screams or the slaps he delivered. All she knew was she didn't want him to hear what she'd heard until the last minute.

"I'm going to do what I should have done years ago. I'm going to fuck you in front of the Murder. Claim you in the way of our ancestors, get that Wolf's stink off your skin, whore," he said, undoing his belt and sliding the leather thing off with a sharp clack.

He wanted a reaction from her. She knew it, but the only thing she could do was smile. Jack's face turned red as he sneered, till suddenly, he heard it too. The sounds of half a dozen motorcycles closing in on them. Suddenly, the air was filled with electricity, magic. Power crackling and covering the Murder like a hushed cloud.

Then they were there. Finally! She exhaled, slumping forward. Her Pack had come for her. He had come for her. Just like she knew he would. The two Crows who'd been holding her up let go, and she fell unceremoniously to her knees, tears streaming down her face.

"Crows to me!" Jack screamed, but most of the Murder had already run away.

The ones who'd initially remained changed their minds real quick when Thor stepped off his gigantic motorcycle. Oh, her mate looked lethal. He wore his jeans and boots, and nothing else but acres of muscles and tattooed skin. Fury rolled off him in waves, and from Derrick and Lucy and the others who made a circle around them.

"You took one of us, Crow. Stole our Enforcer's mate," the Alpha started.

"Big mistake. Huge," Lucy added.

"Now you will see what losing really means," Derrick growled, stepping back with his hand on Lucy as Thor walked forward.

He seemed to get bigger with every step he took. The air around him shimmered, and a swirling mass of black smoke slithered up and down around his body. Nica did not think anyone else could see it, but she sure as heck did. It was terrifying in its power, just as he was mesmerizing in all his masculine beauty.

"She's mine. She was always mi—" Jack didn't get to finish his thought.

Thor raised his hand, like a certain Sith lord in her favorite movie did. With a flick of his wrist, Jack's neck was broken, and the threat he posed to Nica was finally over.

"Angel," Thor growled, coming to her at once.

He ripped her manacles off with his bare hands, lifting her in his arms. The others nodded and clapped, and tears were shed as Lucy approached her and slid a dress over her head. Thor tugged it down the rest of the way, cradling her on his lap as he revved the engine on his bike.

"I'm sorry this is your first ride," he murmured, eyes still black as he looked down at her. Nica shook her head, wrapping her legs around his waist.

I'm not.

She knew the second he realized she'd spoken inside their telepathic link because his eyes went back to normal, and a wide grin split his face right open. Derrick was barking orders, and she heard something about the Council and the Macconwood Pack being on their way to clean up the mess Jack made.

Hopefully, they would reorganize the Murder, set up new leadership, but Nica was not concerned. That was not her life anymore. Her life was with Thor. With her Pack.

"Fuck, angel. I was so worried," he growled, holding her tight. "I didn't think I would get here in time."

"That's nutty because I had no doubt. You saved me again, just like I knew you would," she told him, laughing through tears and holding on for dear life as he pulled out of the trailer park.

"You got that backwards. You've been saving me every day since I met you."

Just like that, Thor's confession melted Nica into a puddle of goo. She didn't think it was possible to love him any more than she already did, but every day, he proved her wrong.

"I love you," she said suddenly, whispering it right into his ear.

Thor revved the engine louder, speeding through the back roads to get back to the Pack House.

I love you, too, he said right into her mind.

Good. Now, take me home, mate.

Thor carried Nica inside, carefully placing her inside the shower stall. Her arm wasn't dislocated this time, just bruised. Her Shifter healing had already kicked in, but he wasn't satisfied until he bathed, dressed, and saw to every single hurt she'd received at the hands of that thankfully now dead motherfucker.

"I'm not glass."

"What?" he asked, laying carefully on his side so as not to jostle her.

"I said, I'm not glass," Nica murmured, her blue eyes flashing up at him from her position in their bed. "I was taken from you today, but I wasn't entirely blameless. I was scared of our connection. I pushed you away. I am so sorry I did that."

"You got nothing to apologize for, angel. I shoulda been more patient. I shoulda explained what I am better. Having the sight makes all those other things way more amped with me. You don't just get a mate, you get all my crazy quirks, too," he confessed sheepishly.

"I love your crazy quirks. I love you."

"I love you, angel. So fucking much," he growled, kissing her head softly.

But Nica was having none of that. His sexy mate crawled over him, spreading her thighs, so she sat with her naked pussy against his belly. He growled, shivering as she leaned down to kiss him fully, her tongue tangling with his.

"Want you, mate. Need you," she whimpered, sliding down so her hot, wet lips stroked his hardened length.

She had him worked up in no time at all. The need to connect with her on this level overpowered his decision to let her rest, and soon she was riding him like the untamed beauty she was. She looked so fucking beautiful. Her curls cascading down her back as she arched, swerving her hips, sucking him deep, so deep, and squeezing him with her tight little channel. Nothing felt better than fucking his mate, and

Thor reveled in knowing she was every bit as wild about him.

"Oh gods, Thor, you feel bigger, deeper, it's too much," she gasped, her movements growing jerky.

"You can take it, angel. You were made to take it," he grunted, holding on to her hips and taking over.

She had his full attention now, riding the cusp of her orgasm like this. Fuck, she was so damn sexy. Her earthy vibe was every bit as delicious as her impossibly strong heart. His hands squeezed her hips, her ass, running over her heavy breasts and back. She was perfection personified. She was all light and pure goodness, the perfect foil for all his darkness. She was everything. And the woman undid him every single time, and she didn't even know it. He was the one riding the edge now.

But there was no way he was going without her.

"Come on, angel. Come for me. Right now," he growled, closing his mouth over the claiming bite he'd given her, scraping the skin with his teeth.

"Thor! Thor! THOR!" she screamed his name, her pussy tightening on him like a vise.

One, two, three more pumps, and he was spewing cum straight into her womb. His dick knotted at the base, traveling up the length until even more of his essence filled her. This orgasm was so intense, Thor might have even passed out for a second or two.

"*Ohmygods,* that was so," she whimpered, both of them a tangled, sticky mess on top of the sheets.

"Yeah, it was," he agreed, kissing her head.

He held her until her breathing steadied, then Thor grabbed a pair of sweats and headed out to the living room. He was not exactly sure how this would work for him, but he took the ancient box and removed the murky ink, shaking it until it started to swirl and glitter with magic. He laid out the bamboo pens side by side as one at a time his Pack mates joined him in the living room.

Of course they would. He'd been pulling on their Pack bonds ever since he felt the urgency to do this now. There were whispers and sniffles, one of the babies cooed, another cried. These were the sounds of life, a good life, and Thor was truly grateful to be a part of it. He worked in silence, allowing those good spirits to fill him, chasing away the shadows that had darkened his sight for too long.

Thor knew the second she walked into the room. Her love was like a beacon in the night, and she shone brightly even from the other world where his spirit currently roamed.

"Thor?" she whispered, as the others parted so she could make way for him.

He smiled then, handing her the first bamboo pen.

"What am I supposed to do?" she whispered, panicked.

Let me in, he whispered into her mind. *Let me in, and I will guide you, show you how to draw the story of us onto my back, mate.*

I don't want to hurt you, she replied, using their telepathic bond. Her love pulsed strongly, and he thanked the gods and the Fates for bringing this woman into his life.

You won't. Just follow my lead, angel.

He was already on his knees, but Thor turned so his back faced Nica. She inhaled a shaky breath, but he was with her all the way. From inside that meta-physical plane where their animals waited together until called, Thor talked Nica through every step of this ancient and most sacred process.

Tears fell from her eyes, and he smiled, knowing they were tears of love and joy as he reached in through their bonds, guiding her hands stroke after stroke as she used magicked ink and one bamboo pen after another to create an image of them on his skin. It took hours, but he was surrounded by his

Pack, and they lent him strength, which he shared with his sweet, brave mate.

There was nothing she couldn't do. Oh, she was still finding her feet, but lucky sonofabitch that he was, Thor was ecstatic he was going to be there to see it all. Every step of the way. He couldn't wait.

"It's done," Nica said with a shaky breath, and Thor released the tension he was holding in his back.

She took a damp rag someone handed her and gently blotted his skin, meeting his eyes in the big mirror someone else had placed in front of them. Congratulations were whispered, and the Pack came forward offering gentle hugs and shoulder pats as they welcomed them as a couple for the first time.

"Don't you wanna see it?" Nica asked, and he felt her curiosity.

He'd already seen it in his mind, but she was so sweet, so excited. He wanted her to tell it to him. To see it through her eyes.

Bright, brave, beautiful mate. Strong woman. Good girl.

"Describe it to me," Thor said, after everyone backed off and he was putting away the ink and pens.

"Okay," she whispered, getting behind him. Her

hands gently touched the periphery of the image and he growled softly, loving the feel of her hands on his body.

"It's our forest, our trail, and there are dozens of leaves falling from the oak tree where we first shifted together," she spoke softly, reverently.

"Demon is sitting on his haunches, big and beautiful, bold as ever. He's looking up at the sky, and I'm in my feathers, flying overhead. Oh my gods, there are two young Ravens with me, Thor," she said, and her voice grew shaky on that part.

Thor turned around and held her in his arms. She was sobbing now, tears of joy he knew cause he felt them too. Thor kissed her head, her temple, her cheeks, her lips, everywhere he could touch, She'd described their future, and it was more than he had ever dreamed.

"Do you want that with me, angel?"

"A family? A future? Yes, oh yes," she replied, kissing him back harder.

"Good. Let's start now."

"Now?"

"Right now, angel."

Thor stood up, taking her with him, and she sighed, wrapping her legs around his waist. It was going to be a long road, but they had each other.

They were the best of each other, and they'd been together through the worst already.

"I love you, Thor."

"I love you too, Nica," he told her before sinking into her sweet body.

His mate was everything he ever dreamed of, and more. She was his anchor to this realm. Nica grounded him, their connection the one thing guaranteed to keep him steady and solid for however long they had on this earth together. And he intended for that to be a very long time.

"Stay," he whispered. "Stay with me."

"Always. I choose you, Thor."

"And I choose you right back, mate."

She was the most important thing. She was everything. And he was going to spend every day of his life showing her. Then Thor kissed her again, and everything else, all rational thought, simply fell away.

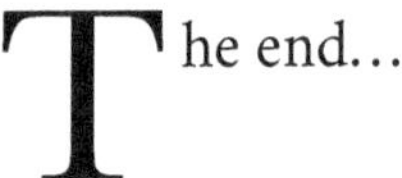he end...

Did you enjoy this Dire Wolf Mates story?

Enjoy the rest of the series today by going to https://www.cdgorri.com/series/dire-wolf-mates
& don't forget to look for Cole's story in Purrfectly F*cked, part of The Maverick Pride tales located here:
https://www.cdgorri.com/series/maverick-pride-tales/!

READING ON A BUDGET?

Hello Readers!

I am so excited to be able to offer you exclusive bundles available only on CDGORRI.COM for readers using my BUY DIRECT option.

Right now, I have several bundles available at a whopping 30% off the listed prices and there are several series bundles to choose from.

Orders will be delivered via BookFunnel email. Just download to your favorite app and READ!

Thank you for buying direct. Have an awesome day!

xoxo,

C.D. Gorri

MOONGATE ISLAND CHRISTMAS CLAIM

She's an overworked executive.
He's a shark with bite.
Together, they jingle all the bells...

A Vampire needing a vacation goes to an island predominantly inhabited by shifters. What could possibly go wrong?

How about an accidental claiming ceremony on Christmas Eve that proves binding by supernatural law? It's not a matter of who bit whom, despite the feuding couple's claims when they take it to the Island Judge.

The real question is whether Adam, a solitary Shark Shifter, and Eve, a Vampire trying to find peace, will end up claimed for life.

Find out in this Moongate Island Christmas tale.

BEWARE... HERE BE DRAGONS!

The Falk Clan Tales began as my stories surrounding four dragon Brothers and how they find their one true mates, but when a long lost brother arrives on the scene, followed by a few more Shifters…what can I say? The more the merrier!

Each Dragon's chest is marked with his rose, the magical link to his heart and his magic. They each have a matching gemstone to go with it.

She's given up on love. But he's just begun.

In The Dragon's Valentine we meet the eldest Falk brother, Callius. He is on a mission to find a Castle and his one true mate, one he can trust with his diamond rose....

His heart is frozen. Can she change his mind about love?

In The Dragon's Christmas Gift our attention shifts to Alexsander, the youngest brother of the four. He has resigned himself to a life alone, until he meets *her*.

Some wounds run deep. Can a Dragon's heart be unbroken?

The Dragon's Heart is the story of Edric Falk who has vowed never to love again, but that changes when he meets his feisty mate, Joselyn Curacao.

She just wants a little fun. He's looking for a lifetime.

We finally meet Nikolai Falk and his sexy Shifter mate in The Dragon's Secret.

She doesn't believe in fairytales, until a Dragon comes knocking on her door.

Meet Castor Falk, the long lost brother of our original four Dragons, and his sassy mate Josette. The Dragon's Treasure is full of adventure and laughs.

Nothing can surprise this six hundred-year-old Dragon, except maybe her.

Devine Graystone meets his match in Sunny Daye, an irrepressible Wolf Shifter with a heart of gold. Read their story in The Dragon's Surprise.

He's a hardcore realist until she dares him to dream.

Nicholas Gravestone doesn't know what to think when he spies Minerva Lykos on the property his Dragon covets. Can this unlikely pair come to a truce? Find out in The Dragon's Dream.

Thanks for reading.

xoxo,

C.D. Gorri

*Dragon Mates & Dragon Mates 2 boxed sets are now available in hardcover, paperback, and ebook.

Have You Met My Bears?

Looking for a Paranormal Romance series that is loads of growly fun?

Meet the Barvale Clan first in the Bear Claw Tales! A complete shifter romance series about 4 brothers who discover and need to win their fated mates!

Followed by two more spin off series, the Barvale Clan Tales and the Barvale Holiday Tales!

No cliffhangers. Steamy PNR fun.
Go and read your next happily ever after today!

Paranormal Romance Books:

Macconwood Pack Novel Series:

Charley's Christmas Wolf: A Macconwood Pack Novel 1

Cat's Howl: A Macconwood Pack Novel 2

Code Wolf: A Macconwood Pack Novel 3

The Witch and The Werewolf: A Macconwood Pack Novel 4

To Claim a Wolf: A Macconwood Pack Novel 5

Conall's Mate: A Macconwood Pack Novel 6

Her Solstice Wolf: A Macconwood Pack Novel 7

Werewolf Fever: A Macconwood Pack Novel 8

Also available in 2 ebook boxed sets

Look for discreet editor paperback and hardcovers

Macconwood Pack Tales Series:

Wolf Bride: The Story of Ailis and Eoghan A

Macconwood Pack Tale 1

Summer Bite: A Macconwood Pack Tale 2

His Winter Mate: A Macconwood Pack Tale 3

Snow Angel: A Macconwood Pack Tale 4

Charley's Baby Surprise: A Macconwood Pack Tale 5

Home for the Howlidays: A Macconwood Pack Tale 6

A Silver Wedding: A Macconwood Pack Tale 7

Mine Furever: A Macconwood Pack Tale 8

A Furry Little Christmas: A Macconwood Pack Tale 9

The Wolf's Winter Wish: A Macconwood Pack Tale 10

Mated to the Werewolf Next Door: A Macconwood Pack Tale 11

Wolf's Scottish Geek: A Macconwood Pack Tale 12

No Otter Lover: A Macconwood Pack Tale 13

Also available in boxed sets:

The Macconwood Pack Tales Volume 1

Shifters Furever: The Macconwood Pack Tales Volume 2

Shifters Furbidden: The Macconwood Pack Tales Volume 3

Shifters Fur Keeps: The Macconwood Pack Tales Volume 4

<u>The Falk Clan Tales:</u>

The Dragon's Valentine: A Falk Clan Novel 1

The Dragon's Christmas Gift: A Falk Clan Novel 2

The Dragon's Heart: A Falk Clan Novel 3

The Dragon's Secret: A Falk Clan Novel 4

The Dragon's Treasure: A Falk Clan Novel 5

The Dragon's Surprise: A Falk Clan Novel 6

The Dragon's Dream: A Falk Clan Novel 7

Dragon Mates: The Falk Clan Series Boxed Set Books 1-4

Dragon Mates 2: The Falk Clan Series Boxed Set Books 5-7

The Bear Claw Tales:

Bearly Breathing: A Bear Claw Tale 1

Bearly There: A Bear Claw Tale 2

Bearly Tamed: A Bear Claw Tale 3

Bearly Mated: A Bear Claw Tale 4

Also available in a boxed set:

The Complete Bear Claw Tales (Books 1-4)

The Barvale Clan Tales:

Polar Opposites: The Barvale Clan Tales 1

Polar Outbreak: The Barvale Clan Tales 2

Polar Compound: A Barvale Clan Tale 3

Polar Curve: A Barvale Clan Tale 4

Also available in a boxed set:

The Barvale Clan Tales (Books 1-4)

<u>Barvale Holiday Tales:</u>

A Bear For Christmas

Hers To Bear

Thank You Beary Much

Bearing Gifts

Bearly Friends

Also available in a boxed set:

The Barvale Holiday Tales (Books 1-3)

<u>Purely Paranormal Romance Books:</u>

Marked by the Devil: Purely Paranormal Romance Books

Mated to the Dragon King: Purely Paranormal Romance Books

Claimed by the Demon: Purely Paranormal Romance Books

Christmas with a Devil, a Dragon King, & a Demon: Purely Paranormal Romance Books

Vampire Lover: Purely Paranormal Romance Books

Grizzly Lover: Purely Paranormal Romance Books

Christmas With Her Chupacabra: Purely Paranormal

Romance Books

Purely Paranormal Romance Books Anthology Volume 1

The Wardens of Terra:

Bound by Air: The Wardens of Terra Book 1

Star Kissed: A Wardens of Terra Short

Waterlocked: The Wardens of Terra Book 2

Moon Kissed: A Wardens of Terra Short

*Now in a boxed set and in audio!

The Maverick Pride Tales:

Purrfectly Mated

Purrfectly Kissed

Purrfectly Trapped

Purrfectly Caught

Purrfectly Naughty

Purrfectly Bound

Purrfectly Paired

Purrfectly Timed

Dire Wolf Mates:

Shake That Sass

Breaking Sass

Pinch of Sass

Kickin' Sass

Love That Sass

Kiss My Sass

<u>Wyvern Protection Unit:</u>

Gift Wrapped Protector: WPU 1

Tempted By Her Protector: WPU 2

Alien Protector: WPU 3

Unexpected Protector: WPU4

<u>Jersey Sure Shifters/EveL Worlds:</u>

Chinchilla and the Devil: A FUCN'A Book

Sammi and the Jersey Bull: A FUCN'A Book

Mouse and the Ball: A FUCN'A Book

Chicken and the Paparazzi: A FUCN'A Book

Jersey Sure Shifters Books 1-3 anthology

<u>The Guardians of Chaos:</u>

Wolf Shield: Guardians of Chaos Book1

Dragon Shield: Guardians of Chaos Book 2

Stallion Shield: Guardians of Chaos Book 3

Panther Shield: Guardians of Chaos 4

Witch Shield: Guardians of Chaos 5

Vampire Shield: Guardians of Chaos 6

Guardians of Chaos Volume 1 Books 1-3

Guardians of Chaos Volume 2 Books 4-6

Twice Mated Tales

Doubly Claimed

Doubly Bound

Doubly Tied

Hearts of Stone Series

Shifter Mountain: Hearts of Stone 1

Shifter City: Hearts of Stone 2

Shifter Village: Hearts of Stone 3

Accidentally Undead Series

Moongate Island Tales

Moongate Island Mate

Moongate Island Christmas Claim

Mated in Hope Falls

Mated By Moonlight

Speed Dating with the Denizens of the Underworld

Ash: Speed Dating with the Denizens of Underworld

Arachne: Speed Dating with the Denizens of Underworld

Asterion: Speed Dating with the Denizens of Underworld

<u>Hungry Fur Love</u>

Hungry Like Her Wolf: Magic and Mayhem Universe

Hungry For Her Bear: Magic and Mayhem Universe

Hungry As Her Python: Magic and Mayhem Universe

<u>Island Stripe Pride</u>

The Tiger King's Christmas Bride

Claiming His Virgin Mate

Tiger Claimed

Tiger Denied

Tiger Rejected

*Tiger Tales Anthology Books 1-3

<u>NYC Shifter Tales</u>

Cuff Linked

Sealed Fate

Virtue Saved

<u>A Howlin' Good Fairytale Retelling</u>

Sweet As Candy

The Grazi Kelly Novel Series

Wolf Moon: A Grazi Kelly Novel Book 1

Hunter Moon: A Grazi Kelly Novel Book 2

Rebel Moon: A Grazi Kelly Novel Book 3

Winter Moon: A Grazi Kelly Novel Book 4

Chasing The Moon: A Grazi Kelly Short 5

Blood Moon: A Grazi Kelly Novel 6

*Get all 6 books NOW AVAILABLE IN A BOXED SET:

The Complete Grazi Kelly Novel Series

The Angela Tanner Files

Casting Magic: The Angela Tanner Files 1

Keeping Magic: The Angela Tanner Files 2

*The Angela Tanner Files Paperback 2 Book omnibus

G'Witches Magical Mysteries Series

Co-written with P. Mattern

G'Witches

G'Witches 2: The Harpy Harbinger

G'Witches 3: Summoning Secrets

Witches of Westwood Academy

Co-written with Gina Kincade

Water Witch

Air Witch

Fire Witch

Earth Witch

Blood Witch

Be sure to check out my BUY DIRECT BUNDLES and get 30% off when you buy available only my website.

EXCERPT FROM PURRFECTLY MATED

How the fuck did I wind up here?

It was all Elissa could do not to slam her face down on the table as she pondered that question for the umpteenth time since leaving her cozy Hoboken apartment to go on this so called date.

"So, babe," the over-stuffed, heavily-cologned, and downright fugly man said.

Her date of the evening looked like something out of a bad sitcom as he tried to lean over the stained tablecloth of the rundown hotel buffet room, he'd driven two hours to get to. Waggling his caterpillar-like eyebrows, he gave her the once over and Elissa's skin crawled.

Oh, hell no.

"I got a room upstairs, you know, for *after*," he told her, nodding his head, and biting his lower lip in a manner she assumed he thought was provocative.

At best, it was nauseating.

FML.

How was this guy Elissa's date for the evening? What had she done to deserve this?

Little Gianni. Yup, that was how he'd introduced himself. And here she was. On a blind date with a guy who had the word 'little' in front of his name.

Well, what did she expect? Roses and champagne? In this economy? She didn't know where Cinder-fucking-ella got her prince, but it sure as fuck wasn't in Jersey.

Elissa could only blame herself for agreeing to go on this blind date. Initially, the whole Little Gianni fiasco had been intended for her roommate.

Wait a second. Scratch that thought.

It *was* all Gretchen's fault. That ungrateful cow!

She tried to play it off like she was some sweet little homegrown maiden. Oh, just wait till Elissa got home. Gretchen was never going to hear the end of it.

She owed Elissa. Big time. Like a whole month of

washing the dishes big time. The rat trap they shared in her hometown of Hoboken was all the two women could afford, and for the most part, they got along just fine.

In fact, they'd grown to be close friends over the three years they'd lived together. It was the only reason she'd ever agreed to this date from Hell.

Elissa sighed and looked over at Little Gianni. Maybe he wasn't all that bad?

"*BEEEELLLLLLLLCHHH!* 'Scuse me, doll. Better out, am I right?"

Gianni winked and Elissa wished for a black hole to open up and swallow her up right through the floor.

OMFG.

The man just burped out loud like he was in a frat boy belting contest, only those days passed him up about thirty years ago.

For fuck's sake. Gretchen, you so owe me.

Elissa cursed her roommate and tried not to groan. But Little Gianni wasn't quite done. The grown ass man lifted his leg and let one rip.

Right. Fucking. There.

Elissa was going to die before the end of the night.

Literally.

This is what you get when you do a friend a favor without asking for details! Idiota!

The voice of her Italian grandmother sounded in her brain. She tried to ignore it, willing herself not to wince at the man while he sucked air, and who knows what else, noisily through his coffee-stained teeth.

Ew. So gross.

That was the perfect word to describe it. The only word, in fact. The entire date was just so fucking gross. She still couldn't believe her sweet little roommate from Iowa, *Gretchen Kaepernick,* she of the wispy hair and baby blues, had set her up with this guy!

What the actual fuck was up with that?

Little Gianni was a slob. Actually, he looked just like her Uncle Nico, and that was not a good thing. Seriously, not good at all.

He wore his hair slicked back in a too tight ponytail that emphasized his rapidly receding hairline. As if that wasn't enough to put her off, he was sporting an enormous paunch. Now, being a curvy girl, Elissa appreciated food and was in no way against men showing the same appreciation.

She liked bigger men. Always had. But bigger did not mean you had to be sloppy. Little Gianni's stomach was literally hanging out from under a tight tan golf shirt that had definitely seen better days.

The man didn't even look like he had ever played a sport of any kind. With it, he wore brown polyester pants that were three inches above his ankles and unbuttoned at the waist.

He didn't look like he tried at all for this date. What kind of guy did that? His shirt collar was bent and wrinkled, and all three buttons were open to his chest, revealing a mat of oily, dark hair and pimples.

Somehow, he'd managed to tuck the back of the shirt in, but the front simply would not hold in that stomach. What worried her more were the tight brown pants.

As he sat back and stretched, she wondered if she should take cover. They looked like they were one bite from exploding off his body. Elissa shuddered at the image.

Please God, if You have an ounce of mercy, don't let that happen, she prayed.

"Hang on, doll, I gotta take this," he said, and turned to answer his cell phone.

It was ringing to the tune of '70s disco music she

hadn't heard since the last family reunion. Her eyes kept going to the huge stain on the front of his shirt. It was a little game she liked to call *what the hell is that.*

Coffee, she guessed.

"Up your ass, Bruno. I gotta have it by Monday," he cursed into the receiver.

Elissa winced at the spectacle he was making of them both. There were only a handful of people there, but still.

Deep breaths.

Ew. Maybe not.

She coughed as the strong body spray, that he'd obviously used a ton of in lieu of a shower, bad move in her opinion, invaded her lungs.

Oh, this was so bad.

Elissa was, by no means, a snob. But this guy looked like he'd stepped out of a bad 1980s mafia spoof film. What's worse, he kept smacking his lips together as he hung up the phone and looked her over from head to chest.

Thank fuck for the table, she thought, wishing she could hide her bosoms from his view.

"Sssssss," he hissed, like it was sexy or something.

She just grimaced. Elissa might be able to forgive a lot of quirks, but she hated mouth noises. Really hated them. It was a super pet peeve of hers. Never mind his totally inappropriate and unwelcomed leer.

She started counting the minutes, willing the date to be over already. Plenty of people would tell her she shouldn't be so choosy, but really? She was not this desperate.

Not yet anyway.

So, she was curvy and a little mouthy too. But was it wrong to want a man with good table manners? Even if men were thin on the ground for someone like her.

As a chef, she'd worked in a lot of restaurants and even as a personal cook for professional couples. She'd seen her fair share of unhappy couples and downright uncomfortable marriages. But as far as she was concerned, all relationships went downhill when good table manners were dismissed.

Good manners were merely a sign that a person was thoughtful and respectful. At least, that was what Nonna had told her. Gianni here had clearly missed that lesson as a child. Elissa had to work not to groan in disgust as he slurped a raw clam down his gullet.

Shudder.

Was there no end to his feeding? That's what it reminded her of. Feeding time at the zoo.

OMG. That was rude, she scolded herself. But it wasn't like she said it out loud.

All she wanted to do was go home. At least she was comfortable. *She'd* worn her softest pair of black leggings for this disaster date, paired with one of her favorite tunics on top.

It was dark green with tiny black buttons down the front and showed just the right amount of cleavage. She'd gone for neat and tidy as opposed to downright sexy.

Good call, in her opinion. Elissa looked perfectly fine for a nice *getting to know you* dinner, which is what she thought she was getting when her roommate asked her to step in for her on a blind date that one of her best client's had set up for her.

Elissa shuddered now, thinking how good old Gianni here would've reacted to the red dress and heels she'd contemplated before checking the weather report.

Gulp.

The lewd man was already salivating, and she was so not having it. Fending off his unwanted advances was not how she wanted to finish the night.

Ew again.

Elissa shivered, slightly chilled despite the fact

they were indoors. It was a cold, gloomy evening, and the forecast called for even more rain later that night. Not at all unusual for this time of year in the Garden State.

November was always chilly in the evenings, rainy too. Elissa tended to run warm, but she was glad she'd brought a jacket with her. Especially since her date refused to turn the heat on in the car.

When she'd asked, he'd looked offended and told her it wasted gas.

Um. Okay.

She checked her phone. It was only seven o'clock, but the two hour drive was still ahead of them. Maybe they could make it home before ten if they left soon.

Ugh. Did he just blow his nose?

"Allergies, doll. Say, you gonna eat that?" he asked before scooping a fry from her dish and swallowing it down.

Elissa was gonna kill her roomie. Gretchen was a hair and nail stylist. A lot of her clients were elderly, and they just loved her. They were always offering to set her up on blind dates with their nephews and grandsons.

Mostly, the sweet old ladies were kind. They swore they could find her curvy roommate the right man, assuming she was single because she was new to town. Well, when Elissa got home tonight, she was going to tell Gretchen she needed to fire the old lady who set this date up from being her client.

Like *ASAP*.

No one who liked Gretchen would've sent her out with this guy. Gianni reached over and touched her hand and Elissa pulled back, reaching for the napkin.

Gross.

"I sure hope you ain't a cold one, doll," he said, shaking his head.

"What?"

"Ain't gonna matter. I know just what you need, doll."

She was still wiping the greasy residue he'd transferred to her skin from the food he ate sans utensils. This was too much. Elissa was beyond uncomfortable with all the leering and bad attempts at innuendo.

Plus, she was starving. One look at the dump he'd taken her to, and she knew she could never eat there. The chef in her wouldn't allow it.

To think they drove two hours for this! She'd practically frozen to death in his maroon Cadillac, listening to a CD of the Rat Pack, while Gianni crooned loudly, and off key, to the music.

Normally, she was a fan of the famous group of legendary singers. Having grown up in Hoboken, she couldn't not be a Sinatra fan. Though, to be honest, Dean Martin had always been her favorite.

Still, Elissa was a firm believer that there were just some people you did not try to imitate. Especially not if you were Little Gianni. While he was belting his heart out, he'd been trying to get his right hand on her thigh. She'd asked him politely to stop.

Twice.

Then she'd been forced to try something a little more drastic. Like spilling her hot tea on the offending hand the third time he'd tried it. Finally, he'd removed his hand from her leg. Not making a fourth attempt, which she was grateful for.

Elissa should've taken that behavior as a sign and gotten out of the car. But no. She'd wanted to do Gretchen a solid. So, against her better judgement, she gave the creep another chance.

Idiota, her grandmother's voice echoed in her brain again.

The old woman had loved her. Elissa knew that without a doubt. She'd raised her after her own parents had passed on in a tragic automobile accident when Elissa was just twelve.

Her grandmother was a no-nonsense kind of lady who dished out priceless wisdom with brutally honest insights. It was the same way she dished out huge bowls of pasta with her amazing meatballs and homemade sauce. Not to mention a side order of back-breaking hugs that Elissa still missed.

Nonna cooked like that all the time. She made a huge pot of sauce every weekend, and she was happy to serve it to Elissa and her teammates and friends, especially after games and tournaments.

Soccer had been her sport of choice, and cooking had soon become her favorite hobby. Her grandmother had encouraged her in both pursuits. Guiding her in one and cheering her on in the other. Elissa still missed her terribly.

"Hey babe, ain't you gonna eat nothin'? You know they charge twenty dollars just to sit down," Little Gianni interrupted her train of thought.

Elissa was forced to turn her mind back to the present, which unfortunately included watching, *and hearing,* him as he sucked on his teeth and stuffed another breaded shrimp down his throat.

"I'm fine," she answered with a polite smile plastered on her face.

Just get home, Lissa. Just get him to take you home.

Elissa closed her eyes when he looked back down at his dish. Thank God for small favors, she mused. At least he was more interested in eating at the moment.

He'd taken her to the rattiest looking hotel and casino she'd ever seen in her life. And the buffet room?

Ew.

Seriously, the place had to be violating at least a dozen health codes. When Gianni had said Atlantic City, she'd thought at least the atmosphere would be exciting. But they were so far from the real glitz and entertainment, they might as well be anywhere else.

She sighed, looking at the plate she'd made for herself. Elissa couldn't even fake an interest in the food. As a chef, it was hard enough to dine out.

She was always judging the food, the service, the ingredients. How could she not? It was her business. And that was when the food was good!

This was not good. Not at all.

She'd been to hospitals that served better food. Old yellow lights buzzed and blinked around the buffet, giving it an abandoned kind of feel. The menu was made up of mostly frozen then fried or baked cuisine.

Reheated actually. It was like a giant TV dinner buffet where every item was previously frozen when already cooked and warmed up in an oven.

It was the kind of food sold cheap at restaurant supply stores in bulk. Yeah, this was much worse than hospital food, in her opinion.

There was a worn carpet on the floor, a handful of scattered tables in the dining room, elevator music on in the background, and the entire place smelled like canned soup.

Not to mention not one of the five people there besides them was under sixty years old.

"Gianni," she said, leaning forward so as not to hurt his feelings.

"I thought you mentioned something about seeing a show tonight. Is it here?"

Please don't be here.

If he was taking her somewhere else, she could beg off and hire a cab to take her home. There was no way she was sitting through anything else with this man. Not now. Not ever.

"Ah, I see, babe, you want some entertainment first, I get it," he snickered loudly, and she blanched.

Whatever he thought was going to happen wasn't. She needed to disabuse him of the notion, and fast.

"Alright, alright. Lemme finish this, babe. Then we'll go up to the room I got for us," he said.

Before she could make sense of the ludicrous statement, he slurped another fried shrimp, don't ask how. Then he grabbed her arm and yanked her from the seat before she could even react.

Elissa tugged on his hold, but the man was immovable. Tossing a five-dollar bill on the table, Little Gianni snatched a toothpick from the hostess stand before dragging her outside.

Great, he was a cheap tipper, too.

All she wanted was to go home. Figuring the best way to do that would probably be to get him to the car, she let him lead the way.

Once inside, she would ask him to drive back to Hoboken so she could wring Gretchen's neck. Fuming, she pulled her arm out of his hand and walked behind him.

The rain was really pouring, and the cheap bastard had refused valet. Elissa ducked her head so she wouldn't get so wet. Of course, the jacket she'd brought was light and had no hood.

Gianni had an umbrella, but he didn't offer to hold it for her, and honestly, she did not relish the idea of getting any closer to him than necessary.

Seriously, not happening.

Now all she had to do was break the news. She had no intention of watching a show or returning to the hotel with him.

What could go wrong?

Grab your copy at https://www.cdgorri.com/books/purrfectly-mated!

About the Author

C.D. Gorri is a USA Today Bestselling author of steamy paranormal romance and urban fantasy. She is the creator of the Grazi Kelly Universe.

Join her mailing list here: https://www.cdgorri.com/newsletter

An avid reader with a profound love for books and literature, when she is not writing or taking care of her family, she can usually be found with a book or tablet in hand. C.D. lives in her home state of New Jersey where many of her characters or stories are based. Her tales are fast paced yet detailed with satisfying conclusions.

If you enjoy powerful heroines and loyal heroes who face relatable problems in supernatural settings, journey into the Grazi Kelly Universe today. You will find sassy, curvy heroines and sexy, love-driven heroes who find their HEAs between the pages. Werewolves, Bears, Dragons, Tigers, Witches, Romani, Lynxes, Foxes, Thunderbirds, Vampires, and many more Shifters and supernatural creatures dwell within her worlds. The most important thing is every mate in this universe is fated, loyal, and true lovers always get their happily ever afters.

Want to know how it all began? Enter the Grazi Kelly Universe with Wolf Moon: A Grazi Kelly Novel or pick up Charley's Christmas Wolf and dive into the Macconwood Pack Novel Series today.

For a complete list of C.D. Gorri's books visit her website here:

https://www.cdgorri.com/complete-book-list/

Thank you and happy reading!

del mare alla stella,
    C.D. Gorri

Follow C.D. Gorri here:
    http://www.cdgorri.com
    https://lynww.facebook.com/Cdgorribooks

https://www.bookbub.com/authors/c-d-gorri
https://twitter.com/cgor22
https://instagram.com/cdgorri/
https://www.goodreads.com/cdgorri
https://www.tiktok.com/@cdgorriauthor

www.ingramcontent.com/pod-product-compliance
Lightning Source LLC
Chambersburg PA
CBHW060345310726
48976CB00003B/731